BEYOND THE RINGS OF SATURN

By
ROBERT MOORE WILLIAMS

ARMCHAIR FICTION & MUSIC
PO Box 4369, Medford, Oregon 97504

*For more information about Armchair Books and products, visit our
website at…*

www.armchairfiction.com

Or email us at…

armchairfiction@yahoo.com

ENIGMA OF AN UNEXPLORED WORLD

Johnson Crane was well known as one of the best interplanetary troubleshooters in the Solar System. Always in demand, his latest assignment had him blasting off to Earth's distant neighbor, the majestic, ringed world of Saturn. But upon landing, Crane found himself stumbling into a hornet's nest of trouble, far more than he ever could have imagined. And when the trouble came in the form of a beautiful dame, it became that much harder to pull the trigger in his own defense.

Robert Moore Williams was known as one of the best writers from the classic pulp fiction era; his specialty being fast-moving sci-fi adventure tales. BEYOND THE RINGS OF SATURN is another fine example of his literary prowess. So buckle up and enjoy the ride!

FOR A COMPLETE SECOND NOVEL, TURN TO PAGE 79

CAST OF CHARACTERS

JOHNSON CRANE

He was a tough undercover agent for the Planetary Government, sent to Saturn to confirm the reports of a fiery new alien creature.

JANE TRUMBELL

She was an officer of Saturian native affairs—until she was taken prisoner by a mad alien who had plans for a planet-wide revolt.

UR-GLUK

As a member of the ruling species of Saturn he was a true telepath. However, he looked more like an alligator who walked upright like a man. Even worse, he hated all Earthlings!

VASTON

His competence as a space commander was exceptional, and everyone on board his space cruiser owed him their life.

CAPTAIN ADAMS

This grizzled old space captain was well past retirement age. He was stubborn, incompetent, and he made far too many mistakes.

GRIMWALD

As the chief engineer, he had the task of repairing his damaged space cruiser—before it crashed into the surface of Saturn!

CHAPTER ONE

"ASTEROID at three o'clock high."

The voice of the technician manning the forward radar lookout position came into the control room of the cruiser, arousing there a frenzy of activity. Anywhere in space an asteroid was dangerous business. Here, inside the rings of Saturn, they were fairly common and all the more dangerous because they were frequent.

In the big, easy chair from which all activities of the ship were controlled, fat Captain Adams hastily punched the button which would connect the big view screen directly in front of him with the radar scanning station in the nose of the ship.

In his agitation, he hit the wrong button. Instead of the bow radar, he got the set in the stern of the cruiser. There flashed on the screen in front of him, a view of the rings of Saturn—rings composed of millions of tiny particles of rock that were the remnants of a moon which once had circled Saturn until smashed in some cosmic collision in the far distant past.

At the captain's mistake, a little prickle of nervousness passed through the men in the control room. There was not a man in the ship who did not know that Captain Adams was over-due for retirement, that he made mistakes.

Vaston, the ship's executive officer and second in command, glanced at the fat captain. The sudden lines of worry were etched on the executive officer's face.

Realizing he had made a mistake, Captain Adams hastily punched another button. This time he got the right one. There flashed on the view screen in front of him a reproduction of a jagged chunk of rock floating serenely through space—the asteroid.

BEYOND THE RINGS OF SATURN

By Robert Moore Williams

The flame beast seemed to hesitate in midair; then suddenly it swooped toward
Ur-Gluk. The Saturian didn't stop to open the door — he took it along with him!

The flame beast brought sure death to its enemies — and little better to its friends!

At the same instant the voice of the forward lookout came again.

"Asteroid not on collision course with us."

The report, plus the vision on the screen, brought instant relief to Captain Adams and to every other man in the control room, except possibly one man at the radio panels. This man was Johnson Crane. Technically, his rating on this cruiser was that of space radioman, first class. If he was anything more than that, no person on the ship had had any intimation of it. A big man, quiet, unobtrusive, there was a hint somewhere about him of hidden strength.

Listening to the report from the forward radar lookout, Crane wondered vaguely if there was anything wrong with it. There was plenty wrong on this ship, he knew. There was also something wrong here in space near the rings of Saturn. He, and some highly placed people in Planetary Government, had been aware of this fact for more than two years. The question was—what? There had been wild reports from freighter captains of something seen here, there had been rumors—

Crane felt a tingle of electricity pass along his skin. It was a mild thing, something like the charge of static electricity a person picked up from walking across a rug on a chilly winter's day. Crane hardly noticed it. What he did notice was the sudden fixed stare that appeared in the eyes of a technician at the plotting table near him.

The man was looking at something. His face was frozen with fear.

Other men in the control room were also looking at something. On their faces was the same frantic look of cold fear.

Crane turned so quickly in his chair, he hardly seemed to move at all. Turned, then instantly stopped turning. Paralysis settled over him. During the space of seconds, he could not move a muscle.

He saw what the other men were seeing.

He saw *it*.

A HUGE hourglass of living flame half as tall as a man hung unsupported in the air of the control room. Alive with glowing colors in the red end of a spectrum, it seemed to have a flaming red core as big as a man's fist, a heart of some kind. Out from this heart of flame, shifting and changing almost too fast for the eye to follow, flowed lines of living flame.

Giving no indication whatsoever that it was coming, it had appeared miraculously here in the control room of the ship. How it had gotten here, Crane had no idea.

The sound that came from it was a soft *brrr*.

There was pandemonium in the control room.

"Where did that thing come from?" a dazed radioman whispered.

"What is it?" a second yelled.

"What does it want?" a third said.

"Get the hell out of here!" a fourth screamed at the flame beast itself, as if he expected it to obey him.

Instead of obeying, it moved toward the man who had screamed the order. The man dived under the table, clawed his way furiously across the room on all fours, like a terror-stricken animal trying to escape, shoved open the door of the control room, bolted through it.

Fat Captain Adams stared from bulging eyes at the flame beast. His mouth hung open. He did not move a muscle.

In his chair at the radio panel, Johnson Crane also sat without moving. Deep down inside of him, he knew one thing, this creature of glowing flame—this was it. This cruiser, wandering on lonely patrol near Saturn on orders from Planetary Government, had been sent here to find this one thing, though no other man on the cruiser knew this except Crane.

Crane had also been sent here to find this thing or to determine if such a thing existed, to check on the wild tales that were being passed by word of mouth through the lanes of space. Probably many men on the ship had heard parts of those tales and had ignored them, not believing that such fantasies could be true.

They would ignore them no longer. Nor would Johnson Crane. The thing he had been sent here to find—had found him.

Very quietly, he slid a hand under the desk support jutting out from the radio panel, pressed hard against a certain spot. A soft, almost inaudible click sounded. No one noticed the click, no one noticed the change in the set. Behind the panels, a special radio transmitter went quietly into operation.

This radio transmitter was something very unusual. Only the men who had ordered it built, the technicians who had assembled it, and Crane knew that the transmitter hidden behind the panels would carry every sound spoken in this control room back across space to Earth itself, where a continuous wire recording would be made of the reception.

When Johnson Crane closed the switch, he was taking action that would automatically inform Planetary Government of every event that happened here.

And plenty was happening.

CAPTAIN ADAMS snatched from its holster the heavy pistol that all space ship captains carried. He fired shot after resounding shot at the hourglass of flame floating in the air.

The thud of the gun rolled through the room.

The heavy lead slugs, designed to knock down a man, seemed to pass through the flame beast without harming it.

It showed no indication whatsoever that it was even in danger.

Adams threw the gun at it, watched without comprehension as the weapon passed straight through the flame creature.

Adams, gasping, fumbled for one of the buttons in front of him. Nobody knew what he had intended to do but there instantly flared over the loudspeaker system of the ship the call to Battle Stations.

Perhaps this was the last sound the crew of this ship was expecting to hear. There had been no war in the Solar System since Saturn had been conquered. No one was expecting war.

The effect on the ship was electric. All over the cruiser, furious activity began. Men, awakening in the bunks, snatched frantically for clothes, failed to find them, and ran half-naked to the blunt-snouted cannons that would hurl explosive atomic charges out through space at any desired target.

Radar scanning stations in nose and stern began searching space for a sight of the enemy. The reports of the operators came back into the control room in the heart of the ship.

"Scanning. No target in sight. Scanning—"

There was no target outside the ship. The object, which had aroused this furious activity, was in the control room itself, in the form of an hourglass of shifting, flaming colors.

The creature swung around the control room.

Without moving a muscle, Crane sat in his chair. "It's making an inspection," was the dazed thought in his mind. He had no idea of the nature of that inspection, of what the creature was looking for or what it wanted.

The freighter captains who had sworn they had seen hourglasses of shining flame appear in their ships had claimed that these visits left dead men behind them.

Dead men…Crane's flesh crawled at the thought. He knew he was probably powerless to prevent the sudden swift appearance of death in this control room unless he could think of something to do. What could he do?

He didn't know. Sometimes all you could do was pray and hope. And keep your eyes open and your wits about you. In this moment, Crane found himself praying.

An inch at a time the flame beast was sliding toward the fat captain. Adams saw it coming. His face worked convulsively. Unable to move, he sat rigid and powerless in his chair.

As the thing approached him, he struck convulsively at it with one hand. The heavy wristwatch that he wore flashed on his arm as he slapped at the creature. The luminous numerals on the dial seemed to glow for an instant.

As if stung, the hourglass of glowing flame jerked away from the blow. Now a sound came from it, an angry burring, like the throttled growl deep in the heart of some animal balked of its prey.

Now it moved with flashing speed straight toward a paralyzed man sitting at the table where the position and course of the ship was being plotted. He struck at it too. Nothing happened. It kept moving toward him.

It settled over him.

The angry burring sound changed in tone, became almost a contented purr, like a cat feeding.

Before the eyes of every person in the room, a man was being destroyed. Everyone knew it. No one knew what to do about it. Vaston was fumbling for something in his pocket.

Johnson Crane acted. He leaped, impulsively, to prevent this man from dying. His left arm was up, aimed at the flame beast. As he struck he saw the numerals of his watch glow with sudden brilliance.

Brrrrr...

The flame beast swirled upward. For an instant, it was a circle of flaming colors in the room. Then the colors vanished. The angry *brrrr* gave way to silence.

The hourglass of flame was gone.

No one knew how it had come into the room; watching it leave, no one knew how it went. Perhaps it flowed through the interstices of the metal, perhaps it slipped into some other dimension.

Johnson Crane was aware of a vast feeling of astonished relief. And an equally vast perplexity. He had done nothing, except strike at the creature. It had fled before him. The man it had attacked had also struck at it. It hadn't fled before that blow.

What had he done to make the flame beast run? Or had it fled from something else, something of which he had no knowledge?

All he knew was that it was gone. He was damned glad of that.

His feeling of relief was swallowed up in the thundering roar that came from the stern of the ship. Crane knew the meaning of the sound. A vent tube had blown out under pressure.

In deep space, this would not be a matter of much consequence. Repairs could be made in a matter of hours.

But this cruiser was not in deep space. It was in close to Saturn, in so near that the gravity of that huge body would pull the ship straight downward.

The cruiser tilted and began to make the long gliding plunge that would end up in an explosive crash on Saturn unless some miracle could be worked in the time remaining.

CHAPTER TWO

THE GIRL had red hair. She also had the slightest skim of freckles showing on her cheeks. The person to whom she was talking—if you could call him a person—had no hair. As to freckles, he actually had a very fine set of them in the form of green mottled scales that he apparently thought very attractive.

He was a member of the ruling species of Saturn. He looked a little like an alligator that had learned to walk on its hind legs but had never quite made up its mind to shed its tail. He had the tail, short and stubby, and in his opinion it was very attractive. Special chairs had been built in the reception room of this Earth administration center of Saturn, so that half-alligators like this one could sit down and be comfortable.

He had a name. It was Ur-Gluk, or something very like that. The girl had never bothered to learn the name exactly. When you used the special language converter that had been devised to aid conversation between Saturians and humans, you didn't always have to get the words exactly right. In this communicator, an element of telepathy seemed to be involved, at least on the Saturian side of the conversation.

The girl's name was Jane Trumbell.

If she had another name back on the Earth from which she had so recently come, it was a secret that she kept entirely to herself. Her title here in Saturn Port was Assistant Administrator of Native Affairs. She was one of hundreds with the same title, all of them working on the perplexing problem of keeping a conquered alien population satisfied. She spoke into the communicator.

"How do your people like the new food laws?"

"Fine. Very fine. Everything you Earth aliens do, we like very much."

It seemed to the girl that the answer came back a little too readily. She had the feeling that Ur-Gluk had thought this answer up beforehand, also that perhaps he was lying to her. How could you tell when a creature that was half alligator was lying to you?

The green colored scales shifted and changed color. The scales indicated something of the emotional state of the creature that owned them.

"That is good," the girl said smoothly. If he was lying, it was a game that two could play. "We must all work together in the interest of peace and harmony." She put real feeling into the words and wondered if that feeling was translated adequately through the language communicator. With every atom of her being, she believed in peace and harmony, in good will toward all life forms. That was one reason she was here, hard at work.

"Peace and harmony?" Ur-Gluk droned back the words at her. "What are these things?"

She was at a loss as to what to say next. How could you explain peace and harmony to a creature that was half-alligator, whose entire life on this rain-soaked planet had been spent in the bitter struggle for survival, who fought his own kind, and every other form of life on Saturn, with a vast and eager ferocity?

"Why—" She stuttered a little, aware that she was confused, and angry with herself because of it.

Crash!

The horned fist of Ur-Gluk came down on the table between them with such force that the stout top splintered.

"You are lying." The words shrilled from the communicator. "You are like all humans. You talk of peace and harmony but what you actually mean to do is to exploit us."

"But—" she stammered. Exploitation was not a part of her scheme of life. She knew the traders, the vast interplanetary enterprises, did actually exploit the natives of all the planets to some degree at least, but that exploitation had a mutual aspect. If they took hard-earned native wealth for their products, they also gave back to the natives tremendous advantages in the form of better products, canned goods, refrigerators, plastics that had a million uses. "There is no real exploitation—"

"Lies, all lies!" the language converter screamed. "You have taken our freedom—"

"But it was in a good cause. You people were threatening

the peace of the whole solar system."

"Had we not the right? Are we not the superior race?" The rage in his voice showed the real source at long last of Ur-Gluk's anger. He, like many other Saturians, had fallen victim to the delusion that they were a superior race.

"Are you the superior race? Prove it." The girl was becoming angry now, both with Ur-Gluk, for shouting such nonsense at her, and at herself, for listening to it.

"I will prove it." The Saturian leaned across the table toward her. "Right now I will prove I am superior to you. You are a spy."

"What?" She gasped the single word.

"You are no simple employee of this administration center. You are a spy, working secretly for Planetary Government."

This secret, she was utterly certain, was known to no one on Saturn except herself. Yet this half-alligator was flinging the words at her as if he was completely certain of what they meant. How had Ur-Gluk known this fact? Had he guessed it? Or did he have secret sources of information?

"I—I don't know what you are talking about."

"You know very well what I am talking about. Your real mission here is to check on how my people are accepting the rule of you humans. Your Planetary Government suspects a revolt is brewing here. You, and many others, I doubt not, have been sent to discover all you can about this revolt. Well, there is one fact you will never report."

"What is that?"

"You will never report to your superiors that we Saturians are ready and prepared to wipe you Earth scum from the face of our planet."

THERE IT was in words, the fatal truth. There was a revolt brewing. Ur-Gluk had just admitted its existence.

Now all she had to do was to report to her superiors. That would be easy. She could walk into the adjoining room and file a report on a wire recorder. Within minutes, her words would be on their way back to Earth.

She rose to her feet. "I don't know what you are talking about." She was quite calm.

"Sit down." Ur-Gluk said.

To her astonished surprise, she did sit down. This one fact startled her more than anything else could have done. What was the matter with her? No one had ever dominated her. No one had ever given orders to her. Except this Saturian alligator.

"But—"

"I will tell you what you are going to do." Ur-Gluk said. "You thought you were going to tell me. But you aren't. I am the one who will do the telling. You are coming with me, this instant, to the hidden laboratories and workshops where the Saturian fleet has been constructed, where the whole revolt has been planned and prepared."

Shock rolled through her. "I will do no such thing."

Ur-Gluk rose. His beady eyes were alive with triumph— and with something else. He moved toward the door that opened outward on to the landing field where his flier was stationed.

"Come," he said.

To her horrified surprise, she found her legs were taking her along behind the Saturian. She was not willing them to walk, they were walking of their own accord.

In that instant she realized—in horrified shock—what must have happened. Ur-Gluk was one of those rare Saturian freaks, a real telepath. All Saturians had touches of telepathic ability; Ur-Gluk had a much larger degree of it. With this ability, he had sensed her thoughts, he had known what her real purpose on Saturn was.

In addition, he had one other ability—he was a hypnotist.

Without her knowledge, he had hypnotized her, done it so quietly and so effectively that she was now completely under his control.

Doubt struck her. Was this true? Could anyone be hypnotized without his knowledge and complete consent? It could not be done on Earth. But this was not Earth, this was Saturn, the ringed planet that swung in grim majesty through space. Such hypnotism might be possible here.

"It is! I have used it." Ur-Gluk's thought came floating into her mind, confirming her worst fears.

Trembling, and with her face white, she found herself going through the door with him.

Outside was a gusty wind that stung her face, and raindrops almost as big as hailstones. They splashed over her, a sudden shower of them, wetting her to the skin, revealing the lithe contours of her perfectly formed body, high breasts, a flat stomach, hips with just the right amount of rounded bulge to them.

The raw air of Saturn stung her nostrils.

Ur-Gluk moved straight toward a Saturian vessel. She followed him, a helpless prisoner.

In this stinging rain and in this biting air, Ur-Gluk was in his element. This was his climate. His skin glowed with a deep, satisfied shade of green. He waddled through the puddles on the landing field as if he liked the feel of water on his feet.

A Saturian guard, posted at the lock of the ship, saluted quickly, and hastily opened the port for them.

Ur-Gluk went in first.

In the door, the girl turned. In her mind was the final desperate thought of flight.

She saw, from the lock of the ship, the vast Earth Administration Center there behind her, hundreds of buildings.

Surely in all that vast concourse, there was somebody who could help her.

Surely, she thought desperately, she could run, screaming, the distance necessary to attract the attention of some human. Over to her left, Earth freighters were unloading. To her right were two destroyers of the fleet.

She could reach them. She would reach them.

"Try it." Ur-Gluk's voice floated into her mind.

She did try it. She found she could turn her head and look. But she could not take a single step in the direction she wanted to go. And she could not scream.

Ur-Gluk had her trapped, hard and fast.

At his command, she moved on into the ship. The lock closed behind her. Vaguely she heard the sound of its closing. Then, quietly, she fainted.

CHAPTER THREE

THE SHIP fell like a shooting star. The planetary mass of Saturn had the vessel in its grip.

Screams of pure panic ripped through the cruiser.

Death lay waiting for every member of the crew, down on the surface of Saturn, death in the form of an explosion that would send red-hot skyrockets of flaming metal soaring through the rain-streaked atmosphere, that would send droplets of human flesh splashing in every direction.

In the control room, fat Captain Adams fiercely pushed the buttons on the control panel in front of him. Answers came back in the form of ringing bells, in the form of voices trying to answer the questions he asked. Adams did not listen long enough to any report to know what had been said to him.

"What happened to that vent tube?" he shouted over the

intercom to the engine room.

"Some imperfection in the fuel…nobody knows…tubes blow sometimes…" the chief engineer was explaining what everybody knew, including Adams.

"Replace it instantly," Adams ordered.

"But that's impossible—"

Adams did not wait to hear what the engineer said. He jabbed the button that connected the view screen in front of him with the bow radar.

There appeared on the screen the gigantic mass of Saturn.

"My God, we're going to crash!" Adams gibbered. His face was blotched.

"Report to space patrol headquarters," he ordered shrilly to Johnson Crane.

"Yes, sir," Crane answered automatically. He turned to the radio panel, started to carry out the order, then realized that he did not have to make a report to the space patrol. The secret transmitter built into the radio set was already carrying a complete report of everything that was happening straight to Planetary Government itself.

Planetary Government issued orders to the space patrol. If the space patrol did not immediately get a report of what was happening here on this cruiser, it did not matter. Planetary Government would handle the report through proper channels.

He did not have to report to the space patrol.

All he had to do was—*act…*

He was in the control room of a ship where a captain half out of his mind was making a dozen different mistakes each moment.

Crane acted with a decision that was characteristic of him. Moving straight across the control room, he slugged Captain Adams on the jaw.

Adams slumped down in the control chair as Crane's fist

crashed against his jaw.

Crane leaned forward against the railing that separated the control chair from the rest of the room, grabbed the fat body and yanked it from the chair. Inwardly he seethed at the high policy which permitted such wrecks as Adams to captain space vessels but as he seethed, he knew that plain ordinary economy measures made such things possible. Competent young men to handle cruisers cost money in the form of a long and expensive training program. Planetary Government simply did not have enough money available to meet all the demands made on it. Hence, it compromised. Hence, incompetents such as Adams occasionally were left in command of cruisers.

JERKING Adams out of the way, Crane settled himself in the control chair. He shoved home the main switch that enabled him to communicate directly with every position in the ship. Now in this moment his voice could go out to all officers in a responsible position and to all members of the crew.

"Johnson Crane, agent, Planetary Government, now assuming control of this ship."

In an emergency such as this, agents of Planetary Government had authority to take over vessels of the space patrol. Every officer and every man on all fighting ships were well aware of this fact. It was written into general orders.

Crane's calm, poised voice went through the ship. The very fact that it was calm and poised helped other men.

Crane waited for the first report to come back to him.

There was a moment of silence. Then a voice came, questioningly, from the engine room. "A PG agent on this ship—"

"Right," Crane said.

"Okay. What are your orders?"

"Tell the chief engineer to take full charge of the engine room and to make all decisions necessary to bring the ship under control for a landing on Saturn."

"The chief engineer? Hell, I'm the chief. Grimwald—"

"Then you must know everything there is to know about handling your own engine room. Handle this emergency as you see fit."

"Do you mean that?"

"It is an order. I have authority to issue such orders. You make the decisions about your own engine room."

"By God, you can bet I will do just that. That damned Adams—" So far the chief engineer could go in criticizing his superior officers, but no farther.

The engine room was the heart of the ship. If the blown vent tube could be repaired even temporarily—

A questioning voice came from the forward lookout. "Sir, not much time is left—"

"Carry on," Crane said.

"Shut up!" a voice said, at his elbow. He turned astonished eyes in the direction of the speaker. Vaston stood there. Vaston was the executive officer who would automatically assume command if something happened to Captain Adams.

Vaston had a face of iron. Hard gray eyes looked straight at Crane, a chin jutted out toward him. Vaston's right hand was pointed straight toward the PG agent.

The hand held a miniature version of a Z-gun.

Crane stared at the weapon. It was a deadly little device. A pellet from this gun would blow a human body to bits. Until this moment, he had not known there was another Z-gun on the ship, except for the one that he carried.

Crane blinked startled eyes at Vaston. "Okay, you've got the gun. What do you want?"

"I only want one thing," Vaston answered. "I heard you

say you were an agent of Planetary Government."

"And so I am."

"Prove it." Vaston shot the two words at him. Crane knew what they meant. Vaston was the man who would take over the ship. Vaston would take it over, with a Z-gun, unless Crane could instantly prove he was what he claimed to be.

"Okay," Crane said. He moved his wristwatch to his lips, breathed gently on it. The crystal had been treated so that it would respond to his breath and to his breath alone. A great deal of chemical research had gone into the construction of that crystal, into making it what it was.

As Crane breathed on it, there came into existence on the surface of the unbreakable crystal a five-pointed star enclosed in a circle—the badge of an agent of Planetary Government.

"Recognize it?" Crane said.

Vaston stared hard at the symbol revealed there. Slowly, his face relaxed. The Z-gun went back into his pocket.

"You are what you claim to be. I accept your taking over command of the ship. What are your orders?"

"My orders?" Crane did not have to think about that. As he had put the chief engineer back in charge in the engine room, his job here was to put this executive officer back into command of the ship. He snapped the switch that communicated with all positions on the ship.

"Crane, PG agent, relinquishing command to executive officer, Vaston."

Crane slid out of the control chair. Vaston, the trace of a grin showing on his rugged face, slipped into the seat Crane had vacated.

"Vaston, executive officer, now taking over ship on orders from PG agent. All previous orders confirmed."

Vaston took over like the competent, efficient officer that he was. The exec knew the ship intimately, knew it far better than Crane. Listening to Vaston issue orders, Crane knew that if anybody could save the ship, Vaston was the man to do the job.

A REPORT came up from the engine room.

"Temporary repairs made on blown vent tube. Blast now functioning."

"Good." Vaston said.

From the rear of the cruiser there came the sweetest of all sounds to the ears of a spaceman: the smooth continuous thrum of engines operating properly.

The mad plunge of the ship was stayed. Like a skittish mare that has finally felt the touch of her master on the reins, the ship seemed to right herself.

Vaston was staring at the view screen. Crane followed the line of the executive officer's gaze, saw with horror what was revealed there.

The ship was already deep inside the atmosphere of Saturn.

Mountains were showing on the view screen. They were hidden by thick mist, swirling rain, but the bulk of them was being revealed by the radar equipment.

Beyond the mountains was a long plateau. Crane caught a glimpse of something that looked like a landing field cut out of the deep jungle of the tableland.

Vaston's face was granite hard. "We're too far down to lift her up before we hit. I'm going to try for a crash landing on or near that cleared space on the plateau."

Ahead was a mountain. Vaston changed the course of the speeding cruiser. The mountain swung by on the left.

The nose of the ship was down. Desperately Vaston was trying to lift it up. He was failing.

"Prepare for crash landing!" his voice rang through the ship. "All hands! Prepare for crash landing."

CHAPTER FOUR

AS SHE STEPPED from the Saturian flier, Jane Trumbell caught her breath. There, moving like a ghost through the mists, was an Earth ship, obviously in distress. She heard the thrum of the drivers, caught a glimpse of the vessel, and knew instantly from its outlines that it was an Earth cruiser. A war ship! If she could get inside, she could report all that she knew about the brewing revolt here on Saturn.

If.

She saw the ship come down on a long glide. She saw it begin to touch the tops of the huge trees that grew here in this Saturian jungle. It plowed a great swath through them. The sound was like a herd of elephants stampeding through a forest. Gigantic trees were snapped off like matches being broken in the fingers of a giant. The girl held her breath.

The ship hit. It bounced. It slewed crazily through the forest. With a great roar of snapping trees, it came to rest near the edge of the Saturian spaceport.

It was down. The stout hull had held. When Earth technicians built a ship to range the lanes of space, they built well. This ship might be an old vessel, but it was solidly built, and it could take punishment. The girl breathed a sigh of pure thanksgiving as it came to rest. There, somewhere in that ship, were human beings. She took a tentative step toward it.

To her amazement, she found she could move of her own free will. She glanced quickly at Ur-Gluk. The Saturian was staring at the crashed ship. The colors of his mottled scales had come down from a brilliant green almost to white. Ur-Gluk, in that moment, came as close as was possible for a Saturian to look like a human who is seeing a ghost.

To Ur-Gluk, the sight of this ship was much more

disconcerting than the sudden appearance of a ghost would be to a human being. An Earth ship, even in a crash landing, near the carefully hidden Saturian landing field and headquarters, was the last sight he wanted to see in his life. He knew how humans worked. If one of their ships crashed, there were certain to be a lot of this strange race around asking why. Also asking what had happened to it. And asking what had happened to the members of the crew.

Humans looked after their own kind. An oath of pure Saturian profanity rolled from Ur-Gluk's mouth.

In that instant, the girl fled silently and quietly across the field toward the crashed ship. She found she could run. Glancing back, she saw that Ur-Gluk had not even noticed her flight. He had his mind on too many other things to think of her.

Behind her, alarm bells jangled. She knew that the Saturians were being alerted, knew also that soon they would be swarming over this crashed Earth ship. If she could only reach the protection of the trees at the edge of the spaceport before they discovered her flight!

She reached the trees. Their green tangle closed in around her. Somewhere directly ahead of her was the ship. She could not see it now, but she knew exactly where it lay. She fought her way toward it. Briars tore her clothes, tore the tender skin beneath. Thorns snagged her. The saw-edged leaves of jungle plants scratched her.

The ship was there directly in front of her. She caught a glimpse of it.

"Help!" she screamed.

Members of the crew were already out of the cruiser. They were too busy congratulating themselves that they were alive to hear a human voice calling in this jungle.

"Help!" yelled the girl again. Still no one heard her. She fought her way through the last tangle of underbrush. The wrecked cruiser lay before her, within her reach. Crying, feeling the throb of misery and of anguish in her heart, she stumbled toward it. She hardly saw the man who turned startled eyes toward her.

"Great God!" Johnson Crane gasped. "A human woman here in this place."

AS SHE CAME toward him, he caught her in his arms. She lay there with her head against his chest, sobbing and gasping.

"What happened to you?" Crane demanded. "What are you doing here?"

She didn't answer, couldn't answer. He let her cry. Suddenly she was talking. "Quick, I've got to tell somebody."

Crane thought resignedly, *They've always got to tell somebody.* Then aloud he said, "Tell what?"

"I'm an agent for Planetary Government." the girl said.

"What?" Crane gasped. That he, should meet a woman here at all was sufficiently startling, that her first words should be that she was a secret agent of PG was almost beyond understanding. Yet he knew that Planetary Government often employed women for this purpose.

"I don't expect you to believe me," she snapped the words at him. "But whether you believe me or not, if you ever get out of here alive, I want you to report to Planetary Government that the Saturians are planning to revolt."

"Lord in Heaven." Crane breathed. "Are you out of your mind? How could the Saturians revolt?"

"I don't know," the girl sobbed. "I mean, I don't know the details. But I know what they are planning. They have built ships. They intend to wipe out Saturn Port in a surprise attack. Then, with their new ships, they intend to defend the planet against any attack Planetary Government can bring against it. In time, they can build up sufficient force to attack

Planetary Government itself."

The words she spoke were so startling to Crane that he shook her, roughly. "You little fool, do you know what you are talking about?"

"I know exactly what I am talking about," the girl answered. Her voice was suddenly calm. She gave Crane the impression that she was listening as she talked, listening for pursuit. Somewhere off in the distance he heard the dang of bells.

"Don't you realize you have landed exactly on the edge of a hidden Saturian space port?" the girl said. "Don't you hear those bells?"

"I hear them."

"They mean pursuit is coming, after me. They mean also that you are in danger. I don't know what they will do to me or what they will do to you. But I know I have to talk fast and that you have to believe me."

"Talk fast, then. I'm listening."

"The Saturians are not only planning to revolt, they not only have built new ships, but they also have some kind of a secret weapon."

"What?" Crane gasped. "What kind of a secret weapon do they have?"

"I don't know," the girl whispered. "I just know that Ur-Gluk let slip the thought of a secret weapon. I don't have any idea what it is. But it exists, and it is real. Please, you must believe me. Also you must get my information back to Planetary Government as quickly as possible."

Crane hesitated. This girl was stark raving crazy, from terror or from something else. He had no idea what had actually happened to her but he could recognize terror when he saw it. There were no secret weapons. There were only new developments of old ideas. "Get yourself under control. You are acting like an idiot."

He shook her again, then stopped shaking her as one single horrible picture popped into his mind.

THE PICTURE that came into his mind was the memory of the thing he had seen back there in space, the thing that had come into the control room of the cruiser that lay behind him, the horrible monstrosity that had almost wrecked this ship.

What if that monstrosity he had seen with his own eyes was actually the secret weapon of the Saturians?

What if they had made some really new discovery and had been testing its effectiveness against Earth ships in the lanes of space?

What if this monstrosity was actually some new discovery and was under the control of the Saturians? Perhaps it might be directed by very high frequency radio waves, sent to its destination, then recalled at the will of the operator.

"But I don't know of any device that could be used like that," he whispered.

"Like what?" the girl answered.

He shook his head savagely. "Now I'm crazy," he snapped at her. "I saw something come into this ship, almost wreck it, knock it out of control."

"What did you see?" the girl said.

"I don't know what I saw," he answered. "All I know is, I saw something. What the hell it actually was, I intend to find out, if I can."

"One thing you can do that would certainly help is to get the report through to headquarters of Planetary Government," the girl said.

"Why don't you do it?" he answered.

"Because—" Her face changed. A blankness crept over it. "Because— Oh, I can't say it."

She backed away from him, then turned abruptly and

began to run. What had happened she knew very well. Ur-Gluk had discovered she had fled. The Saturian had resumed his telepathic hypnotic control of her.

"Come here!" Crane shouted.

She fled into the dripping forest and lost herself there. She didn't know it but she was running straight to Ur-Gluk, who was coming through the jungle growth with a force of Saturian soldiery at his heels.

She ran straight to Ur-Gluk before she knew she was near him.

"Uh!" the Saturian grunted, at the sight of her.

She cringed away from him.

"Take her, keep her out of sight," Ur-Gluk snapped, to the Saturian major in charge of the group of soldiers.

Trumbell found herself in charge of two Saturians who were smaller replicas of Ur-Gluk. They were soldiers, armed with heavy swords that were more like battleaxes than any Earth weapon the girl had ever seen. The heavy axes were used for fighting at close quarters. There are few things the Saturians like better than to go into close combat, swinging these heavy axes, their fierce battle cries sounding from hoarse throats.

In addition, the two soldiers escorting Trumbell away from the ship were armed with some stubby little weapon that looked a lot like a machine gun, but obviously wasn't.

One blessed fact was sure in her mind. Ur-Gluk had released his hypnotic control of her. She was again able to act of her own will.

All she had to outwit were two Saturians. If she could get away from them, she could eventually get back to the ship, get back to the presence of human beings.

If.

CHAPTER FIVE

AS CRANE realized the girl was running from him, he started after her. She slid into the green tangle. As elusive as a vanishing ghost, she was gone.

"Hey!" he yelled. "Come back here."

There was no answer. He shouted again, louder. From behind him, Vaston called, wanting to know what was wrong. He ignored the officer. Whoever and whatever this girl was, she was important. What was this mad story she had babbled? Why had she run away from him?

The fact that she had fled at all was utterly confusing to Crane. Secret agents of Planetary Government did not run away from danger. They were a carefully selected, tough minded, tough muscled lot. Certainly this was true of the men: perhaps however the women were not quite so tough minded as the male of the species. Nobody had ever been able to predict quite what a woman would do in a crisis.

Crane was already out of sight of the ship.

"Hey! Where are you?"

He did not get an answer from the girl. Instead he heard the crashing of underbrush which announced the approach of something—he did not know what. Before he could move, the underbrush opened in front of him. A Saturian soldier stood there. At the sight of the human, the Saturian lifted the heavy axe that he carried, and prepared himself to charge.

Crane stood poised. The Saturian charged. Crane ducked, slid to one side. The lifted axe that had been aimed at his head knocked bark from a heavy tree.

The startled Saturian soldier turned, seeking his elusive prey. Crane's hand was already in his pocket, his fingers around the butt of the Z-gun that he carried there. This Z-gun was the weapon of last resort so far as PG agents were concerned. Crane did not want to use it, would not use it if he had another choice.

The soldier started toward him again. Crane's finger crooked around the firing trigger of the Z-gun.

A harsh command rang out.

The soldier stopped. He came rigidly to attention. Crane turned quickly. A whole party of Saturians had fought their way through the underbrush. The command to the solider to stop his attack had come from their leader.

CRANE FACED them. The leader was big, even for a Saturian. He stood looking at the human. Crane stared straight back at him. It was always difficult to tell what a Saturian was thinking, or even if he was thinking, but this leader seemed to be especially difficult to read. Only the keen bright eyes showed he was even alive.

Crane did not look at the bright, glowing eyes. Instead he looked at a spot directly between them. It was an old trick with him, one he used unconsciously. So far as the Saturian could tell, Crane was looking him straight in the eye. Crane knew he wasn't, knew also that as long as he did not look this creature straight in the eye, but only appeared to do so, there was no chance that the Saturian might slip up on him with some of the telepathic hypnotism these alligator monsters sometimes used.

Crane felt something probing at his mind. The hunch that came up in him then was that this monster, somehow or other, was trying to read his thoughts. His first amazed idea was that this mind-reading stunt was impossible.

If it was possible that this Saturian monster was trying to read his mind, Crane had an answer. He forced himself to think of the crashed ship behind him, of the simple fact that it had crashed, giving no reason for the crash other than engine failure. He also forced himself to think of the situation directly facing him, that he was looking a Saturian in the eye and was a little worried as to what might happen next.

But not much worried. If he appeared to be too worried, the Saturian might make a shrewd guess as to the cause of that worry.

There, in that moment, without Crane fully realizing what was happening, he was locked in battle with a shrewd and wary and very intelligent antagonist.

If Ur-Gluk could read his mind, could get from it too much information, Crane and all the other occupants of the ship might be dead within hours. If Ur-Gluk could hypnotize him, by telepathy, as he had hypnotized the girl, Ur-Gluk would be in complete command of the situation.

If.

Crane felt sweat oozing from him. He was fighting something, he did not know what. Deep layers of his mind shrieked warnings at him.

Sweat oozed out of him as he kept these voices hidden within him. He did not move. He stood still, facing the impossible, waiting for it to happen, whatever it was.

Little by little, it began to happen. The fingers of thought probing through his mind began to go away. Suddenly Ur-Gluk dropped his gaze. The Saturian's deep green color began to change, to drop down the scale toward white.

Crane was not quite sure of it, but he thought something of a shudder passed over this half alligator.

Ur-Gluk was shaken. In this moment, Ur-Gluk had run up against what seemed to him to be the impossible, a human being he could not control and could not understand.

Ur-Gluk made a gesture. A Saturian hastily brought forward a portable communicator.

In that simple gesture, Ur-Gluk began to fight for time. If he could not read the mind of this human, then he had to talk to him over the communicator. Perhaps, via the communicator, he could get the information he wanted.

Ur-Gluk was not licked; he was simply baffled. He did not know what to do.

Crane was likewise baffled. Like Ur-Gluk, he did not know what to do.

"ARE YOU IN trouble?" Ur-Gluk's voice came over the communicator. "We saw the ship crash——"

"And naturally you came to help us," Crane said, quickly. In his mind was the memory that the first Saturian soldier had tried to kill him, also in his mind was the disturbing fact that this monster had tried to seize control of him. Also was the memory of the girl. It didn't seem to Johnson Crane in this moment that these Saturians had actually come here to help.

"Well——" Ur-Gluk's communicated thought and voice-tones faded out.

"Well, what?" Crane said. "We need some help. Had some trouble in the drive rooms and made a forced landing. You will be well paid if you help us. But, in case you are considering attacking us, the ship is armed with atomic cannon in good operating order." Desperately Crane hoped the last was true.

If the cannon were not in good order, they soon would be. Trust Vaston for that.

"But, certainly, we want to help," Ur-Gluk said. He said it twice. He said it again. "You have only to command our poor services. The best we have is yours."

"Good," Crane said. "We will accept such help as we need." Inwardly, he had deep reservations as to the real nature of the help this Saturian monstrosity intended to offer. In Crane's secret opinion, which he kept well hid from any stray telepathic pickup, what Ur-Gluk wanted most to offer was a knife in the back. Or one of those Saturian axes over the head of a human who happened to stand in his way.

"What are you doing here?" Ur-Gluk said. "The ship is there." He pointed through the green tangle. "You are here." Again the eyes sought Crane's vision. Again Crane looked at a spot directly between the two flaming optics of the Saturian.

"I heard you coming," the human answered, easily and indifferently. Crane had no intention now of revealing that he had been chasing a girl. The girl was a bit that fitted somewhere into a much vaster puzzle, a picture puzzle that moved perhaps across a cosmic stage.

"Oh. You heard us coming?" Ur-Gluk said. The way the words came out of the communicator formed a question. Again Crane felt the groping fingers trying to work their way into his mind. He clamped down hard control.

"Sure," Crane answered. "Everybody within a mile must have heard the noise you alligators made when you came thundering through the jungle."

"Uh!" Ur-Gluk twisted. To Crane, it was obvious that the Saturian was uncertain and in doubt. Crane could almost read the mind of Ur-Gluk from his actions. Ur-Gluk was worrying about this sense of hearing that humans possessed. Did humans hear sounds that Saturians couldn't hear? Did this perhaps mean that humans might possibly possess other senses of which the Saturians were unaware?

"Are you perhaps an officer of the ship?" Ur-Gluk asked.

"No. Just a radio man."

"Do you humans dare to send such unimportant underlings to meet us?" Anger flared through the communicator. Ur-Gluk didn't like the idea of being met by anyone less potent than the commanding officer.

"Sure," Crane answered. "The exec, when he heard the noise your bunch made, sent the first man he found. I happened to be that man. There was no offense intended."

"Uh. No offense."

UR-GLUK didn't like that idea, either. If these crazy humans could send just anybody to meet such an important Saturian as he was— Well, in that case, they must feel utterly secure. If they felt secure, perhaps they *were* secure. In which case, it behooved a smart Saturian like Ur-Gluk to proceed with extreme caution, to feel his way along until he could make up his mind.

"If you would like to return to the ship with me—" Crane said.

"Naturally," Ur-Gluk grunted. "Of course I will return to the ship with you. Likewise I will bring with me this guard detail which you see here." He nodded toward the silently watching Saturians.

Crane shrugged again. He turned. The instant his back was turned, he might get a thrown battle-axe in his brain. He might also get a charge from those stubby little weapons the Saturians were carrying.

Turning his back now and walking toward the ship was like walking into the face of certain death. Crane knew it, knew also that he had no choice, that the slightest show of weakness on his part, the smallest indication of insecurity, would bring the ravening horde down upon him.

As he moved away, he slipped his hand carelessly into the pocket that held the Z-gun. Also, he listened for the sounds that soon would, or would not, come from behind him.

Which would it be, the almost silent swish of a thrown axe, the blast of a gun—or would it be the tramp of heavy feet following him?

He felt his heartbeat pick up as he waited for the sound that would give him the answer to—life or death?

CHAPTER SIX

THE GIRL was held prisoner. She had thought she could outwit two stupid Saturian soldiers, she had attempted to run, and had been caught almost before she had taken three steps. From then on, one of the soldiers had carried her. They had placed her in a locked, barred cell located somewhere underground. She did not know where she was. She did not know what was happening.

All she knew was that time was passing. A day, two days, three days passed. Food was brought to her at irregular intervals. The only way she could tell that time was passing at all was by the fact that the door was opened occasionally and food and water were shoved in at her.

During this time, she almost went mad. She wondered if her message that the Saturians were planning to revolt had been delivered to anybody who would take it along to Planetary Government.

Had the man she had talked to understood what she was saying?

Or had the ship been attacked by the Saturians and every human aboard massacred?

She paced the floor of her cell, back and forth, repeating an endless round of aimless steps. When she was too tired to take another step, she fell sobbing on the rude bunk in one corner of the room. She was asleep when the guards finally came for her.

Half-carrying, half-dragging Jane Trumbell, they took her up flights of steps, so many she lost count of them. They brought her to a door, opened it, and shoved her through.

She was pushed into a room that was well furnished, according to Saturian standards. Trumbell paid no attention to the furnishings. There was only one thing in this room that caught and held her attention—a man.

It was the same man she had talked to outside the wrecked ship. She stared at him, hardly able to believe her eyes, hardly able to realize he was there in person, alive, seemingly unhurt. He was rising to his feet. His face was puzzled, perhaps a little worried. But, in spite of the worry on it, this was a kind face, maybe the kindest face she had ever seen.

She fled to this man, fell sobbing into his arms. He let her cry. "I'm Johnson Crane," he said softly. "I've been looking for you."

Deep down inside of her she was aware that it felt good to know that this man had been looking for her. "I'm Jane Trumbell," she whispered. "What—what happened to the ship?"

"It's ready to leave," Crane answered. "Vaston, the executive officer, happens to be something of a genius. He brought the ship down safely, major repairs have been completed." He was telling the truth. What he did not tell her was that a ring of Saturian soldiers was now guarding the ship.

The Saturians were there ostensibly to "protect" the ship from dangerous animal life in the jungle. Their actual purpose, both Crane and Vaston guessed, was to prevent the ship from taking off until Ur-Gluk was ready for it to leave.

Or for it not to leave, depending on which way Ur-Gluk made up his mind.

UR-GLUK was being very wary, and very cautious. Crane had warned both officers and crew to be constantly on guard against any mind reading attempts via Saturian telepathy as operated by Ur-Gluk. So far as Crane knew, Ur-Gluk had not succeeded in getting any information from the crew except what the Saturian's eyes had given him. Nor any information about the ship, either. No Saturian had been permitted to enter the damaged vessel.

"Did you—did you—?" The girl's heart was in the words she was trying to say. What she wanted to ask was whether or not Crane had succeeded in passing along to Planetary Government the information she had given him about the Saturian secret weapon and the revolt on the ringed planet.

As she started to speak she felt Ur-Gluk's probing thought tendrils enter her mind.

The fact paralyzed her. Ur-Gluk again was reading her mind. She knew instantly what this fact meant. Her meeting with Crane was a trap Ur-Gluk had set.

Ur-Gluk was trying to get information from her. Just as he had gotten information from her back in Saturn Port, without her knowledge, he was again planning to strip her secrets from her.

If she opened her mouth, if she even thought such things, Ur-Gluk would know instantly that she had told Crane about the revolt.

Ur-Gluk would destroy both her and Crane.

The thought froze her mind and body. She could not move. She could only stare at Crane, hoping somehow that he understood what had happened.

Crane saw the change come about in her.

"What's wrong?" he said. "Why—uh—nothing," she whispered.

"But something is wrong," he insisted. "I can see it in your face and in your eyes."

"Nothing, nothing," she answered. Her voice was a whimper, a little whisper of sibilant sound.

He caught her shoulders. "Tell me!"

"But I can't tell you. If I do—"

She did not finish the sentence. Instead, she hung limply in his arms.

With a growl, he caught her up. He did not know what

was wrong with this girl, but he knew there was a damned competent doctor back on the ship.

"I'm taking you back to the ship with me," he said.

It was the most welcome sound she had ever heard.

Carrying the girl, Crane turned to the door by which he had entered. Neither Ur-Gluk nor anybody else would dare try to stop him.

He lifted the heavy latch on the door, started to open it.

The door did not swing open.

He shoved against it.

It did not give.

Horror rising in his heart, he read the door had been quietly locked behind him.

They were trapped.

He swung away from the door. A sound caught his ears. Across the room another door was opening. Crane stared at it. Under the girl's body his fingers moved swiftly to slip the Z-gun from his pocket. He hid the gun from sight.

The door opened.

Ur-Gluk stood there.

"THE SATURIAN looked more like a monster than ever. His green scales were glowing with a vivid green color. His alligator jaws hung half-open. His eyes were gleaming.

In his hand, he held one of the stubby little weapons of the Saturians. No axe, no sword, just this little weapon. Behind him came two other Saturians, carrying the inevitable communicator.

"Drop the human!" Ur-Gluk shouted. His eyes were fixed on Crane with feverish intensity.

Crane looked directly between these glaring eyes.

"To hell with you," he said quietly.

"Ah?" The gasp that came from the communicator indicated astonishment.

"I said to hell with you." Crane repeated. To the Saturian, hell was a meaningless word. However, the communicator, picking up Crane's voice, would translate hell into some word that would carry the equivalent meaning to Ur-Gluk.

Ur-Gluk turned even greener with both anger and rising fear. He shoved forward the little weapon he held.

"This is a new weapon, a secret weapon," he said menacingly. "It will blow you, and the girl too, into bits of bloody human flesh."

Crane caught his breath. There was some substance to the girl's wild story about the Saturian's possessing a secret weapon. They actually had such a weapon.

But would Ur-Gluk use it? Crane clutched the Z-gun he held. Should he shoot now, and destroy this Saturian overlord, or should he wait? Sweat was pouring from him.

"Perhaps you do not believe in the power of this weapon." Ur-Gluk said, almost smiling. "I will show you what it will do."

He swung it, at the nearest of the two Saturians who had entered the room with him.

There was a soft *phut* from the weapon. There was a much louder *phut* from the Saturian as he was literally torn into shreds of bloody flesh. Green colored blood splashed the walls of the room. The stricken Saturian crumpled into a formless mound of dead cells.

"You see," Ur-Gluk said boastfully. This was his triumph. No human would dare reject the evidence of his own eyes. Ur-Gluk watched Crane, waiting for the dazed moment to come to the human when he could seize control of him.

Crane looked utterly astonished. But his astonishment was from a different cause than what Ur-Gluk thought.

"Is that your secret weapon?" Crane gasped.

"It is." Ur-Gluk answered.

"Do you know *what* that weapon is?" Crane asked.

"Yes. I mean—"

"It just happens to be a modification of the Z-gun that we humans developed long ago," Crane answered. "I don't know the whole story but probably some spy stole old blueprints for the development of the Z-gun, and sold them to your scientists. Your secret weapon, Ur-Gluk, happens to be a device that we have developed for a very specialized use, to protect important messengers, secret agents, and very important people in Planetary Government."

The Saturian stood frozen. In the space of a moment, he changed color at least three times.

"I don't believe it," he scowled, at last. "You are lying. You lie like all other members of the human species. The truth is not in you. You are attempting to trick me—" There was more of it but it went off into shrill imprecations that were beyond the power of the communicator to translate.

Crane quietly let the girl sag to the floor. Now, for the first time, the Z-gun he held was revealed.

Ur-Gluk stared at the weapon the human held.

"I'll show you how the real Z-gun operates," the agent said.

He pressed the trigger.

The explosion that rolled through the room was at least five times as loud as had been the roar from the gun Ur-Gluk had used. Crane had aimed at the opposite wall.

The stout masonry there was ripped to pieces as a gaping hole appeared in the wall.

Outside was the Saturian night, the mists and the rain.

In bewildered consternation, Ur-Gluk turned his head to stare at the damage.

As the Saturian stared, appalled, Crane said, quietly.

"Drop the gun you're holding or you will get the next shot."

As Crane watched, his finger ready on the trigger, Ur-Gluk's green color faded swiftly to a shade of white.

CHAPTER SEVEN

UR-GLUK dropped the weapon he carried. It clattered on the floor as it fell and the Saturian collapsed into the nearest heavy chair, for once completely oblivious of any possible damage to his precious tail.

The second Saturian, who had helped carry in the communicator, was looking from the smashed body of his companion, to the hole in the wall. Then his beady eyes were roving toward Ur-Gluk. His color was almost white too. A shiver ran over him. Suddenly he toppled over in a faint.

Crane stared at him. "Hell on wheels, a Saturian fainting," he thought. So far as he knew, the scaled superior life form that ruled the Ringed Planet had never been known to faint.

Ur-Gluk was making a tremendous effort to rally himself. Some color was creeping back into his hide.

"Shall we talk?" Crane asked softly.

"What about?"

"About this revolt you have been planning," Crane said.

"What revolt? Who told you that?" Angry green colored the alligator scales.

"You did."

"I did?"

"The instant we met, I knew you were trying to hide something. Also, Planetary Government has rather adequate sources of information. It is their job to know exactly what is going on all over the solar system. It is impossible to hide preparations for a full-scale revolt. You Saturians have been very carefully watched, for years."

At his feet, the girl stirred. Without relaxing his gaze from Ur-Gluk, he knelt. One hand held the Z-gun, the other sought her pulse. It was strong and firm. He heard a little whisper of sound come from her. "Oh, I'm all right again.

I've got my own mind back. He—he had me under some sort of hypnotic control that he worked by telepathy. Also, he could read my mind."

"Shhh," Crane whispered. "Control your thoughts. Think of something pleasant, maybe something that you want to do very much. That way, he won't be able to get anything important out of your mind. Also, never look him directly in the eye. Look between his eyes."

"What? You seem to know—"

"Actually, I don't know. I'm only doing a lot of guessing."

"But a guess may not be right."

"Sometimes we have to work on a guess and a bluff. I'm doing exactly that right now."

"A bluff?"

"Sure. And you can help me."

"Me? How?"

"By putting up as good a bluff as I am doing. Both of us will know we are bluffing, but Ur-Gluk won't know it. Are you with me?"

He didn't look down at her and hence could not see the sudden gleam in her eyes, a look which said that she was with him, no matter where he went or what he did. He felt her fingers seek his free hand. He helped her to her feet.

UR-GLUK, watching with wary suspicion, again attempted control of her mind. The probing telepathic tendrils met a feeling that baffled him utterly. This girl was happy. She was thinking of something far away, some scene that Ur-Gluk did not begin to understand.

If she was happy, she could not be in danger. So Ur-Gluk reasoned.

The simple fact, which Ur-Gluk missed completely, was that this girl was falling in love. Nobody had ever succeeded in explaining to a Saturian the meaning of love.

The color of the Saturian, which had been rising again toward green; faded back toward white. To him, love was beyond the understanding and he was afraid of things he could neither understand nor control.

"My suggestion would be that you cooperate fully with Planetary Government in developing Saturn," Crane said.

"But you humans exploit us!" Ur-Gluk exploded.

"Yes," Crane answered, instantly. "But the exploitation is mutual, we give as good as we get."

"You lie."

"Well, make up your mind which you would rather be: exploited the way humans exploit you—or blown to bits."

Ur-Gluk wriggled in his chair, hating the ultimatum and the human who had given it.

"You have some gadgets that you probably think are important," Crane continued. "The modification of the Z-gun, probably some ships—no doubt you also have some carefully laid plans. What good are your ships and your so-called secret weapon when we know about them—?"

"That is exactly the question," Ur-Gluk snorted. "You and this girl know about them. But does your government know?"

"I assure you—"

"And you may be lying."

"Lying with this in my hand?" the human answered.

"You can kill me," the Saturian said. "But someone else will take my place. And, even if you kill me, you can not save yourselves." Triumph again was glittering in the alligator eyes. "While you have been talking here, I have been in contact with my second in command, by telepathy."

Crane gasped in sudden alarm.

"Your inferior human mind cannot comprehend the use of telepathy. My second in command is gathering a squad. Even if you kill me, you will never succeed in getting back to your ship."

Ur-Gluk rose ponderously from his chair.

"So shoot. Shoot and suffer death yourself."

No doubt, to the Saturian mind, Ur-Gluk was acting exactly like a hero. Crane, in this moment, had no trouble at all in understanding that under the hide of this half alligator there beat a heart that was fiercely loyal to his own kind.

"We've got to do something," the girl whispered. "We'll run for it. Out the hole you blew in the wall."

"But—"

"He'll never catch us. If he starts after us, shoot him."

CRANE FROZE. Out of the corner of his eyes, he was aware that beyond the hole something was moving in the rain-washed Saturian night—an object that looked a little like a wandering, vaguely moving fireball.

Rousing memories, the sight sent chills over his body.

"Hell no!" he gasped.

The girl had stopped. "What?" she said.

"That thing." Crane said, pointing toward the hole in the window.

"All I see is a moving light—"

"If it's the wrong kind of light, that may be too much to see."

Involuntarily Crane had turned his complete attention toward the hole. Ur-Gluk stopped hastily and scooped the fallen gun from the floor. Crane had forced him to drop this weapon. Now he had it back in his possession. He folded both hands behind his back, waited impassively.

The moving light came closer to the window. Crane stared at it. He felt his heart muscles contract, felt the sweat begin to gather in the palms of his hands.

The girl glanced at him. "What is it? What's wrong?"

He did not answer. He hardly heard her speak. His eyes

were glued on the moving light. It was coming closer and closer to the hole he had blown in the wall.

He saw it clearly now.

His heart almost stopped beating as recognition came.

An hourglass of gleaming flame, half as tall as a man, alive with glowing colors. Not the green of the Saturian, not the tanned, honest brown of a human face, but red, orange, a vague pink, all flowing and shifting almost too fast for the eye to follow them.

"The flame beast!" Crane gasped.

Here it was again, the thing that had suddenly appeared in the ship out near the rings of Saturn. At one time, Crane had thought that perhaps this was actually the secret weapon of the Saturians. Now he knew that the weapon on which Ur-Gluk had placed his reliance was actually only a modification of the Z-gun.

Or had he been mistaken? Ur-Gluk had said he was sending for his second-in-command.

Was this flame beast the thing he had sent for?

It came through the hole in the wall, hung glowing in the air. It burred softly, a sound that was a little like the purr of some strange cat.

The Z-gun in Crane's hand exploded. This was the ultimate weapon. At this close range he could not miss. Firing, he waited for the explosion.

The explosion came out in the Saturian night. The pellet from the Z-gun had passed completely through the creature.

Z-gun bullets needed to hit something to explode. This creature offered no resistance.

Against the flame beast, the Z-gun was useless.

Crane stood paralyzed. Out of the corner of his eyes, he was aware of Ur-Gluk. The Saturian had turned dead white, the color of abject fear.

Crane knew that Ur-Gluk had never sent for this thing.

The Saturian had not known it was coming. This flame-beast was definitely not something Ur-Gluk had been expecting. It moved toward Ur-Gluk.

The Saturian leader threw both hands over his head and bolted for the door. He did not try to open the door first, he ran straight through it, headfirst. The crash of splintering panels, of breaking hinges was loud in the room.

The flame beast hung in the air. It seemed to be making up its mind.

Then, slowly and gently, it started to follow Ur-Gluk.

The room was empty.

"Quick, through that hole in the wall and out of here!" Crane gasped.

CHAPTER EIGHT

LIKE TWO harried ghosts, the man and woman slipped through the hole and into the rain-streaked Saturian night. Through a break in the clouds, the rings of Saturn's were occasionally visible above them, millions of asteroids circling this grim and foreboding planet.

"The ship is this way." Crane said. "Run!" He clutched her hand. Part of the time, he was literally jerking her along. She ran like a deer following him; when she slipped, he pulled her forward.

They were in a cluster of buildings hidden under the tall jungle trees. This was the secret Saturian headquarters and it had been well camouflaged. It was also well guarded.

Somewhere ahead of them a Saturian grunted. Crane stopped short, caught and held the girl. The Z-gun was focused on the spot from which the sound had come.

"A sentinel," Crane whispered.

They waited, hardly daring to breathe. The sentinel moved on, following his beat. They slipped past behind him.

They were in the jungle. Behind them, in the secret Saturian headquarters, alarm bells were ringing. Crane thought grimly that perhaps the Saturians were having their hands full with the weird monster that had come from nowhere out of the dark night. There would probably be a violent uproar in this Saturian hideout until that creature was repulsed. What was this creature that had come out of the night? At the thought, a startling idea occurred to Johnson Crane.

"Good Lord, is it possible that that thing actually is—" he muttered.

"*What* thing is what?" the girl said.

"I may have stumbled on to the real explanation of what that hourglass of flame actually is. And also I may have discovered a way to defeat it." Grimness crept into Crane's voice. He recalled how the hourglass of flame had appeared in the ship and how it had acted, how it had started toward Captain Adams—and then had moved away from an up—thrust arm. In his mind was the glimmering of an idea as he fitted the factors together.

It was an idea that he could not even believe himself.

"We've got to get to the ship and blast off," he said. "I've got to check this idea of mine against the files of Planetary Government."

"You seem to have access to a lot of information about Planetary Government," the girl said.

"Haven't I told you? I'm actually a secret agent, working for Planetary Government."

"Heavens," the girl whispered. "So am I."

"No!" Crane gasped. "I considered the possibility, but I never once believed that two secret agents could run into each other, with each of them failing to recognize the other, but with both of them working on different aspects of the same problem."

"If it's happened once in history, it has happened a thousand times," the girl said. "If you don't believe me, I'll give you all the secret signs."

"I'll take you on faith for right now," Crane answered. "You can show me your secret signs when both of us have time. Right now we've got to get to that ship, and get away from here."

AGAIN THEY hurried through the dark, rain washed jungle. Behind them, the growing uproar from the secret Saturian headquarters faded into the night.

They moved ahead until Crane caught a glimpse of a dim light. "The ship," he whispered. There was a ring of Saturian guards around the cruiser. He had come out through them, stating that his purpose was to call on Ur-Gluk, at that august creature's direct request. At the mere mention of Ur-Gluk's name, the guards had passed him through without question.

Would they pass him back through? Also, would they pass him through when he had a girl with him? He had gone out alone, now he was coming back with someone else. What would the Saturian guard captain think of that?

"We're going to walk up to that guard captain as if we owned him," Crane said. "If he doesn't let us through—"

"Bluffing again," Trumbell said.

"Sometimes you've gotta do it." Crane answered. "Are you with me?"

"I'm with you." Her voice was firm, it left no doubt that she was with this man in whatever he tried to do. Crane squeezed her hand. "Sometime remind me to tell you what a swell person you are," he said.

Together they slipped through the jungle, together they walked straight up to the big tent the Saturians had erected to shelter the captain of the guard and his staff.

The guard captain came out of his tent to inspect them.

The inevitable communicator was already set up in a panel under the canopy of the tent.

"What is this?" the captain growled.

"*This* person got lost from the ship when we landed," Crane answered, gesturing toward the girl. "I'm bringing her back."

"But I have no instructions—"

"Your instructions are on the way," Crane answered. "Ur-Gluk himself had ordered that she be allowed to return to the ship with me. She is in urgent need of adequate medical care…"

"Oh, Ur-Gluk. Yes, yes, of course. Pass on." The startled captain almost saluted as the two humans walked past him.

"See how easy it is," Crane said. He glanced sideways at the girl, saw that she wasn't listening, that she had hardly heard him. Her eyes were dropping, her step was lagging. Seeing her torn clothes, guessing at the terrific strain she must have been under for many days, he knew she was about to faint. Catching her in his arms, he ran toward the ship.

The guards on the alert there were human. They recognized Crane and admitted him without question. Still carrying the girl, he ran forward to the hospital rooms. There a young doctor was poring over a book on space medicine. His name was Gale.

"What on Earth have you got there?" Dr. Gale gasped, rising.

"A human woman. I think she needs rest and care. But that's your field. You take over."

"Sure thing. Put her here." Gale gestured toward the examining table in the next room.

"Take good care of her, doc." Crane said as he went quietly out the door.

HE LEFT the hospital rooms with the comfortable knowledge that he had left this woman in competent professional hands.

"Where's the exec?" Crane shouted, at an ensign who was passing.

"In the control room, sir." This ensign had heard Crane's announcement over the loudspeaker when the PG agent had taken over the ship after the failure of Captain Adams. He knew his manners. "Shall I call him, sir?"

"Never mind," Crane said. He raced to the control room. Vaston was there with a group of officers. At the sight of Crane, he instantly stopped his conversation and came forward.

"We're ready to take off, sir," Vaston said. "Emergency rig."

"Don't startle me like this," Crane answered. "I didn't think you would be ready to take off for days yet. How did you work this miracle?"

"I turned the engine room over to the engineer," Vaston answered. "He worked the miracle. We have only been waiting your return and your orders."

"Orders? Oh, sure. Technically I am fully in command of this ship. I had forgotten it. Okay, Vaston, here are your orders. Take off as soon as possible."

"That will be in a matter of minutes," Vast on answered. "Our friends outside may be a little surprised."

"Let them be." Crane answered. If some of the Saturian soldiers got their scales singed in the backwash of an atomic blast, it would teach them a badly needed lesson not to get too close to ships from Earth.

Vaston slid easily and comfortably into the control chair. He seemed to fit there, to belong in this spot. Under his fingers, switches closed almost of their own accord. Lights glowed. "Clear for take-off," Vaston said.

Crane, slipping down into the nearest chair now strapped himself in against the acceleration. He could almost feel the ship begin to pick up life as Vaston's orders went smoothly and efficiently into effect. Suddenly there came the soft, insistent throb of the take-off warning.

Probably every person on the ship held his breath. Starting slowly, but accelerating as rapidly as the human body could stand, the ship swung into the air. Possibly the startled Saturian soldiers tried to take measures to stop the take-off. No one on the ship knew, or cared.

The ship was in flight and the surface of Saturn was slipping swiftly away below them.

"Space radio has been yaking for you," Vaston said, when the ship was clear.

Crane roused himself. "Space radio?" He glanced over at his old position where he had worked as a radio operator when this ship had blasted off. It was filled now, by a youthful rating whom he vaguely remembered as being one of the other radio men. The kid seemed to be doing a good job.

"Lot of code stuff," Vaston said. "Stuff that isn't even in our code books."

"I see," Crane said. Planetary Government had one cipher that every agent was required to memorize and to carry around in his head. Probably this code that Vaston mentioned was actually this cipher. In any event, he had no time to bother to try to decipher it. Unstrapping himself, he rose to his feet.

"I am going to use your radio equipment for a while," he said, to Vaston. "What I am going to talk about is the business of no other man in this control room."

"Right." Vaston's eyes roved over the men in the room. "Personally, I am not going to be able to hear a word that is said in this conversation. I don't want even to think that one of you may overhear it."

His eyes lashed the men. Nods went around the room. Crane slipped into the chair that had been hastily vacated by the rating. His fingers went under the panel. The switch was still on, the circuits still functioning.

"Johnson Crane reporting."

ALTHOUGH this radio equipment was carrying full details on everything that was happening in the control room, Crane was in full charge of the situation until he reported in. This was standard operating procedure in the Planetary Government espionage system. Efforts might be made to reach him via space radio but this hidden communication system would not be used for that purpose unless the agent himself requested it.

Crane patiently waited for an answer. Even at the speed of light, time would be needed for this message to reach Planetary Government headquarters, to be acted upon, and for orders to be issued and to reach him here in the forlorn sky above Saturn.

Then a voice was speaking across the reaches of space.

"To: Johnson Crane. Space static has prevented reception from you of more than fragmentary reports. Impossible to evaluate your information as yet."

There was a pause. Crane, wondering desperately what was coming next, could almost hear paper rustling as the operator on the other end shuffled through the reports in front of him. The voice went on:

"Additional data for your information and guidance. Freighter completely gutted by hourglass of flame you describe. Two other ships report similar attacks near rings of Saturn."

"What?" Crane gasped.

The voice went heedlessly on.

"Some menace seems lodged in or near the rings of Saturn. Unable to evaluate nature or origin of this menace. Two cruisers, five destroyers, have been dispatched and are proceeding at full speed to you. You can expect radio contact with them in matter of hours. You will take charge of this fleet.

"You are also in full charge of entire operation.

"Find menace and destroy it."

The voice went into silence.

Crane sat staring at the radio panels. He was too stunned to speak.

He had expected help from Planetary Government. He had hoped to use their files to check his ideas as to the origin and the nature of the hourglass of flame.

Instead, he had been placed in full charge of the job of finding and destroying the menace.

It seemed to him in that moment to be a job beyond the ability of every human being alive.

CHAPTER NINE

TWENTY-FOUR hours later, radio contact was made with the approaching fleet. The message was relayed to Crane down in the engine room, where he was driving the chief engineer and all the spare technicians on the ship mildly nuts working out the details of what they considered to be an utterly fantastic idea. Grimwald, the chief engineer, had snorted his disgust a dozen times. But Grimwald was working. So were all the others. When Crane gave orders to work, men usually obeyed them.

The message that contact had been made with the approaching fleet came down from Vaston. Crane went up to the control room to get the details. Vaston was wooden faced.

"Admiral Harkness reported. He asked our position. I gave it to him."

"Good," Crane said. "What else?"

Vaston's face became grimmer. "Admiral Harkness said he had lost one destroyer, and had had one cruiser crippled by excessive loss of manpower, by attack from scores of these flame beasts we are looking for."

CRANE digested the information in silence. He glanced at the view screens. There, displayed in all their brilliance, were the rings of Saturn.

"I want you to set all lookouts on the watch for an asteroid that moves under its own power," Crane said.

Vaston stared at him as if he did not believe his ears. "How can an asteroid move under its own power? They move in orbits."

"I know," Crane answered. "But I have a hunch that perhaps there is one asteroid somewhere near Saturn that moves under its own power."

"Sounds impossible," the exec said, softly.

"It may be," Crane said. "But just before we had our first contact with that hourglass of flame, the lookouts reported an asteroid near us. Now, suppose that object was actually a space ship designed to look like an asteroid—"

"But why?" Vaston said.

"To conceal it, for one reason. If you wanted to find a hiding place for a space ship in an asteroid belt, what better way to do the job than to make the ship look like an asteroid?"

Vaston's eyes were suddenly thoughtful. "I grant that part. But who would want to find a hiding place in an asteroid belt?"

"I don't know who, I just know that apparently something has appeared in this asteroid belt, something that looks like an hourglass of living flame. Since I don't know much about the real nature of this hourglass of flame, I can only guess as to its motives and it purposes. I do not doubt it has its own secret motivations. However, my orders are to find and to destroy it. And the thing I want you to do is to search for an asteroid that seems capable of moving under its own power, and which may be the secret hiding place of the flaming hourglasses."

"I'll do it." Vaston said. Replacing the puzzled bewilderment in his eyes was a quick eagerness. "It may be a hell of a job to find one single asteroid in the millions that are here, but we'll find it, if it exists." As he finished speaking, Vaston began to issue orders to the lookouts.

A few minutes later, the radio was calling again, for Crane. This time the message was from Admiral Harkness. "My orders are to report to you. I am so reporting. We will meet you at your instructions. Meanwhile, I wish to report the conclusion of my medical examiners regarding the men killed aboard both the cruiser and the destroyer."

"Go ahead," Crane said.

"This is it. The flaming creatures that came aboard the ships, seemed to kill the crew by devouring the life force within them. My examiners say there is a subtle force in every man that keeps him going: they also say that this force is electrical in nature. The flame creatures devour this force. I pass that on to you for what it is worth—"

"It's worth plenty," Crane answered. "We will proceed to a meeting as soon as a course can be plotted. In the meantime, there is a possibility that these flame creatures may be hiding in a space ship designed to look like an asteroid. My orders are to blast out of the sky any asteroid that seems to appear near you and to be moving under its own power."

Crane signed off. He knew he left a puzzled Admiral out there under the rings of Saturn. But he also knew that this

Admiral would carry out any orders given to him. Crane hastened back to the engine room.

THE SPACE suits were already coming out of the special ovens that had been rigged up. The ovens had been set up in such a way that each space suit passed near the atomic engines in operation. Each suit thus received a slight charge of radioactivity. Back on Earth, radioactive isotopes had been manufactured in this way ever since the discovery of atomic power. Space suits normally were designed to protect their wearer not only from the cold of space but also from the effect of dangerous radiation.

These suits, however, had been put through a process that made them slightly radioactive.

Dr. Gale looked up from the adapted Geiger counter he was using on each suit as it came out of the oven. "It's my guess that a human can wear these suits for thirty days with no danger. But why are you having them made radioactive?"

"On the strength of a hunch and a prayer," Crane answered. He grinned at the girl who was helping Dr. Gale. Jane Trumbell looked wan and shaken but she was operating under her own power. She smiled back at him.

Crane moved on to the bench where the technicians had assembled and were already testing the weapon.

Improvised from parts of the ship's stores, the weapon was a crude, clumsy-looking gadget that looked a little like a sub-machine gun made by amateur gunsmiths. However, this weapon did not fire slugs—it fired puffs of smoke.

Crane, his face grim, watched the tests. The weapon was mounted in a test rack and it was aimed at a target, a radiation counter. One of the technicians pressed the trigger. Out from the flaring muzzle of this odd gun shot a hard-driven ball of smoke.

The ball of smoke hit the radiation counter. The meter

jumped over into the red, then fell back as the smoke passed it.

"Radioactivity of the smoke discharge, point nine three seven," a technician said to Crane.

"Good," Crane said. Humans could stand indefinitely this amount of radioactivity. Trumbell moved up and stood beside Crane.

"Radioactive space suits and a gun that shoots radioactive smoke?" the girl said. "I wish I knew what you are trying to do."

"I wish I was sure of what I am trying to do," the PG agent answered.

Suddenly the call to battle stations sounded through the ship.

Crane snatched the weapon from the test rack. "Make a dozen more like it, as fast as you can!" he shouted. The girl following him, he ran for the control room.

Before they reached it, they heard the thud of an atomic cannon firing.

In the control room, Vaston looked up as they entered. He pointed toward the view screen. "There's your damned asteroid!" he shouted. "We're trying to knock it out of the sky!"

Looming in the view screen was what looked like a tremendous chunk of jagged rock. There were thousands like it wandering erratically through and around the rings of Saturn.

"We missed it with the first shot," Vaston said. "Ah, there goes the second."

Again the thud of an atomic cannon firing rolled through the cruiser.

ON THE view screen, they saw the explosion that followed. The bursting charge struck the asteroid a glancing blow. The explosion that mushroomed up was so bright it hurt the eyes even when watched through a radar view screen.

The asteroid rolled under the massive impact of the explosion. Jagged chunks of rock flew away from it. Heat in the intensity of millions of degrees had been generated against the surface of this wandering fragment of what appeared to be a tremendous chunk of jagged rock. Volatized stone spurted outward in molten drops of fine spray which cooled instantly in this airless space to microscopic mist.

Crane glued his eyes on the view screen. Without knowing it, he was holding his breath.

Was this the asteroid he had thought existed here? Was it the hidden source from which the flaming hourglasses sprang? Or was it just a chunk of rock?

Something burred in the control room.

Jane Trumbell screamed.

Crane jerked his eyes away from the view screen.

There, in the control room, was an hourglass of living flame. How it had gotten there, he did not know; apparently these creatures possessed some sort of ability to slip into another dimension and thus enter a closed area without the necessity of going through any kind of opening. All he knew was that it was there. And that it was moving straight toward him.

He jerked up the muzzle of the improvised weapon that he carried, pressed the trigger.

The ball of smoke shot out.

It struck the exact center of the hourglass of flame, struck where the vague orange color was turning into a glowing spot of deepest red, struck what might well be the heart of this monstrosity.

As if the smoke did no damage whatsoever, the flaming

hourglass kept moving toward Crane. The sound that came from it jumped a notch up the scale as the smoke hit it, there was no other indication that it had been touched.

Crane's dazed thought was that the smoke had only made it angry.

He felt again the electric tingle pass through his skin as the creature neared him. He caught a glimpse of Trumbell's white face beside him. He fired the second shot.

Again the ball of boiling smoke shot into the heart of the creature.

What happened then took place almost too fast for the eye to follow.

The heart of glowing red inside the creature seemed suddenly to swell to larger size. Then it collapsed to a pinpoint of intense scarlet.

The burring sound changed. A split second earlier, it had throbbed with anger. Now, somehow, it had a note of pain in it as if this creature had been hurt.

The hourglass of flame was no longer moving toward Crane. It was hanging in the air as if somehow it had lost the power to move of its own accord.

Crane fired the third shot.

Again the ball of smoke struck home. The burring sound roared up again. The creature moved. Like a stricken wild animal, it dashed madly around the control room.

The burring sound leaped a final notch up the scale.

The creature vanished.

In the control room the only sound was the frightened breathing of startled men.

Crane thought in dazed relief: "Those damned things actually can't stand radioactivity."

In that instant, he knew his wild hunch had been correct, knew also that he had found a weapon with which to combat these hourglasses of living flame.

He had won! The thought was like a tonic to his mind. Exultation leaped up in him.

"Look!" Vaston yelled.

Crane turned again to the view screen. There, plainly displayed, was the asteroid.

"It's moving under its own power." Vaston said. "It's a hidden space ship."

Plainly visible on the view screen, the asteroid was righting itself. The force of the atomic explosion had sent it rolling. It was rolling no longer. Instead it was obviously under control.

And it was fleeing from the ship.

Crane breathed a sigh of pure relief.

The thud of a cannon rolled through the cruiser. The shell exploded far behind the rapid-accelerating asteroid.

At the explosion, the asteroid suddenly took up a course that any experienced space cruiser executive officer would instantly recognize.

"Evasive action!" Vaston yelled.

Crude and cumbersome in many of its movements, the asteroid was dodging and ducking, trying to avoid those atomic explosions that were taking place behind it.

"Pursue that asteroid!" Crane yelled. "Don't let it get away."

Vaston, grimly busy with the control switches in front of him, was already changing the course of the ship.

A white-faced junior officer burst into the control. "Hey! There's another one of those flame beasts here in the ship!"

CHAPTER TEN

OUTSIDE the door of the control room a man was down. He lay without moving on the plastic covered steel floor.

Hunched over him, feeding off him, was another hourglass of living flame.

Radioactive smoke boiled from the gun in Crane's hands. It struck the creature again and again. The flame beast lifted, tried to move toward the PG agent.

Another smoke ring struck it.

Crane watched the hourglass of living flame try to flee. In his mind was the grim thought that this one was not going to escape, if he could do anything to prevent it. The gun puffed its balls of smoke, innocent-looking balls they were to a human being, but to this flame beast, they were nearly as deadly as the slug from a Z-gun was to a man.

The flame beast hung in the air. A violent surge of colors ran through it. Suddenly it was drifting, floundering, falling. Something had gone wrong inside of it. It struck the floor of the corridor, hung there an instant. The colors in it faded, faded, faded—and were gone.

A tracery of lines as fine as spider webs remained upright for a moment. Then this web faltered and fell in upon itself. There remained on the tough plastic floor a web of moisture.

Johnson Crane was probably the first man to see one of these creatures die. Now he knew one fact that he had never really known before: these flame beasts could be destroyed.

On the floor, the man stirred and tried to sit up. All he could do was wave his hand. Some vital energy had been sucked out of him. Getting it back would be a problem for Dr. Gale.

"Take it easy, fella," Crane said. "Just lie there. We'll get to you as soon as we can."

Crane raced again to the engine rooms. For an instant, he was almost afraid to enter. Suppose he should find these flame beasts in here too? Shoving into the engine rooms, he found his fears were without foundation. Men in here were working. So near these atomic engines, no hourglass of flame would ever appear. To the flame beasts, this engine room was "hot."

Dr. Gale looked up from his inspection of the space suits. "Man up there in the corridor outside the control room who needs your help," Crane said.

The medico was gone almost before the words had left Crane's mouth.

"I want five volunteers."

Crane got them instantly. "Into space suits," he ordered. In a matter of minutes, he had five men inside the suits.

"In these suits, you will be safe from the flame beasts," he said. Arming them with the stubby-smoke guns, he stationed them around the ship in positions where a sudden call for help from any quarter would find one of these men ready to answer it instantly.

"Now, let another flame beast appear," he thought.

The ship was accelerating and changing course. The thud of the atomic cannons was sounding again.

CRANE ENTERED the control just in time to see one of the atomic shells strike the fleeing asteroid.

The explosion was cataclysmic.

The view screen revealed a vast mass of machinery of some kind spewing outward from the center of the asteroid. It also revealed the astonishing fact that the huge chunk of jagged rock was a real asteroid.

"They bored into the center of an asteroid and installed driving machinery." Vaston gasped.

"They'll never bore into that asteroid again." Crane answered.

Apparently the shell had penetrated to the core of the asteroid. The great chunk of rock was torn into hundreds of pieces. Leaping out from it, flashing upward through airless space, were—flame beasts. They were trying to flee from an atomic explosion.

That explosion not only generated millions of degrees of heat, it also generated the whole gamut of "hot" radiation that goes along with an atomic explosion, the alpha, beta, gamma rays, along with many others. Some of these rays, possibly all of them, were a deadly poison to the flame beasts.

The vast holocaust in the sky of space revealed the flame creatures dying by the hundreds. They tried to flee. Who can flee from the blast of an atom bomb?

In the control room of the cruiser, the awed humans watched the sky of space light up, watched the flame creatures die, watched the holocaust die down.

"That's that." Vaston said. "Now to dodge the shower of fragments from that explosion."

Already the meteor warning bells were ringing. The ship, which had been pursuing the asteroid, swung away from the collision course with the fragments. The clanging of the warning bells died into a quiet murmur.

"Do you suppose that was the only asteroid those flame beasts have taken over?" Vaston said, softly.

Crane grimaced. "Let's not think about that right now," he said.

The ship turned quietly in space. For an hour, the crew rested. Food was served. Down in the engine room, more space suits were made slightly radioactive. More of the improvised weapons were made ready. Men were wary and watchful and restless. They thought the flame creatures had been conquered. But who could be sure when dealing with some totally unknown life-form such as these weird hourglasses of flame?

The crew was suddenly aware that space was just outside the ship. The kind of space that leered at men. They were aware that they were under the rings of Saturn—where almost anything could happen. Men started to whistle, and stopped short. Laughter came up in sudden bursts, then was still.

The ship swung around to make her rendezvous with the approaching fleet.

Then space radio was again yapping for Crane.

"Harkness reporting. We're being attacked by three asteroids. Our situation is desperate and we must have immediate help."

Before Crane could answer, the voice coming over the radio went into sudden silence. He snapped a question back across space. There was no answer.

In the flagship of Admiral Harkness, the transmitter had gone off.

What had happened to the fleet? No one knew. With the fleet's radio out of operation, there was no way to find out.

"We're on course to meet them," Vaston said. "We ought to make contact almost immediately." He swung the view screen to the forward radar equipment, scanned the vastness of space for a sight of the approaching vessels.

Minutes passed while the cruiser was accelerated. The minutes grew into an hour.

"There!" Vaston said. "I caught a glimpse of the ships."

Crane and the executive officer strained their eyes staring at the view screen. Pips of light were visible. They enlarged rapidly, became two destroyers and a cruiser.

Three other pips of light became something else, became three jagged chunks of rock.

Three asteroids in motion.

CHAPTER ELEVEN

TWO OF THE asteroids were small, not much larger than destroyers. The third was larger than the biggest space wagon that Planetary Government had ever put into the skies.

The asteroids were circling the fleet. The destroyers and the cruisers were firing, sporadically. Out in space in the vicinity of the three asteroids, atomic explosions were taking place. The aim of the gunners was erratic, the explosions were missing their targets.

"Look at that." Vaston whispered.

As the cruiser neared the scene of battle, other objects were becoming visible.

Circling what remained of the fleet were hundreds of the flame beasts. Like wolves around helpless prey, the hourglasses of flame were swinging in swift orbits.

"They're too close in for the ships to fire upon them." Crane said. "Also, they're too close to the vessels for us to fire. What in the hell are we going to do now?"

"We can fire on the asteroids." Vaston said.

"Done!" Crane shouted. "If we can't get at the flame beasts themselves, we can at least destroy their nests."

From the nose of the cruiser, in response to Vaston's order, came the thud of an atomic cannon. It was aimed at the nearest asteroid. It missed. The second hit.

The nearest asteroid exploded in a blinding burst of glittering flame.

"One down." Crane said. Two more were left to go. But the first shot that had destroyed the nearest asteroid had been a lucky hit and he knew it. What about the other two? What about—?

The PG agent was staring at the screen. As if the explosion of the asteroid had been a signal, the flame creatures had left off their circling of the helpless cruiser and the two destroyers.

They had started toward the new ship that was approaching. They seemed to recognize in it a source of danger.

"By God, when they started toward us, they made a

mistake." Crane said confidently. "Now we can get at them. Fire into that swarm as it approaches."

As long as the flame creatures had remained close to the remnants of the fleet, they had been safe from fire, both from the helpless vessels and from the cruiser.

Again the atomic cannon thudded. This time the shell exploded in the midst of the approaching swarm of flame beasts. An atomic mushroom boiled upward and was dissipated. Wild spots of flame gyrated through black space.

"Got part of them!" Vaston said.

"The rest are still coming."

The flame creatures seemed to move with fantastic speed. Before a second shot could be fired into them, they had flashed in from space and were circling the cruiser.

Like balls of witchfire appearing out of nowhere, they popped up inside the ship. Alarm bells began to ring.

THE FLAME creatures had been having things pretty much their own way inside the vessels of the fleet. Appearing inside the hull of this cruiser, they expected to find the same situation: helpless, frightened humans who fled screaming before them, men who did not understand them and were afraid of them, running men, men paralyzed by fear.

Swirling inside the ship, they danced up and down the corridors.

Shouts of fighting men answered them.

"Get that damned fireball over there."

"Got him!"

"There's another one."

"I'll take care of him."

Instead of finding running men, the flame creatures met puffs of radioactive smoke. Within that smoke was death.

Two of the flame beasts appeared in the control room. Jane Trumbell, looking very grim in the smallest space suit aboard the ship, took care of one of them. She fired balls of radioactive smoke. The flame creature swirled away from her, and vanished. "I can lick 'em too!" she yelled.

Crane was at work on the second flame beast that had appeared in the control room. It vanished.

In the control chair, the wooden-faced Vaston took a new grip on life. Instantly he began checking all positions on the ship.

"All clear here."

"No flame creatures in the after-section."

"Two destroyed in the nose."

Excited shouts answered Vaston's queries. All reports added up to the same answer. "All clear!"

The cruiser was clear of the menace. But outside, in space, the flame creatures circled, wary and watchful, as if they were considering some new plan of attack.

In the far distance, the smaller asteroid was changing course. Vaston was following that shift of direction with a wary eye. Shells were exploding around this asteroid but as yet none had taken effect.

"That son-of-a-gun looks to me like he is getting ready to ram." Vaston said. The ragged edge of nerves frayed almost to the breaking point sounded in the exec's voice. He moved the button that put him into contact with the engine room. "Stand by for fast evasive action."

"Ready." Grimwald's voice came back.

On the control panel in front of Vaston, a signal light glowed red: the stern lookout at the radar set calling for emergency attention. Vaston snapped the view screen to that position. The voice of the lookout came quickly. "Fleet coming up from Saturn."

Crane heard the words without realizing their possible meaning. He turned quickly to the view screen.

There, visible against the dark bulk of the gloomy planet

that lay so far below them, were rapidly enlarging pips of light. Five ships, coming upward.

"Those are not ships of our space fleet." Vaston whispered.

"But what other ships could possibly be here?" Crane gritted. As he asked the question, the answer popped into his mind. "That damned Ur-Gluk."

"They're Saturian ships all right," Vaston spoke. "But where in the hell did the Saturians get ships? Those are war craft. They're not permitted to have fighting vessels. The treaty they made decided all that long ago."

"They didn't keep their treaty." Crane answered. "Ur-Gluk has been building ships, in secret. He's been planning an attack, to wipe out human control of Saturn. He's picked the worst possible moment to launch his blow."

Of all the things that could possibly have happened, this seemed to be the worst. Circling outside the ship were the flame beasts. Off in the distance an asteroid was being maneuvered to ram. The rocky mass would tear through the fragile hull of the cruiser like a thrown stone going through a pane of glass.

Back farther still was a huge asteroid, the heart and the core of the flame creatures.

THE EARTH fleet lay helpless even to protect itself. The ships were barely under way. Firing had stopped. The vessels moved as if the only guiding force within them was the automatic equipment that kept them on course even after their human operators had all died or had fled precipitately from the controls.

In this crisis, the Saturian fleet was attacking.

"The asteroid is the source of immediate danger." Crane spoke from between dry lips. "It will reach us before Ur-Gluk comes within firing range. Concentrate on the asteroid."

Vaston turned the view screen again. His face grew grim as he watched. The asteroid was looming bigger with each passing moment. There was no longer any doubt but that the creatures manning the driving machinery inside of it intended to ram.

The fore-guns were firing at it. A shell grazed it.

It kept coming.

Bigger and bigger it loomed on the screen. It had been the size of a baseball, then it was as big as a basketball. With tornadic speed it became the size of a mountain.

Vaston waited.

The asteroid loomed even bigger on the screen.

Very gently the executive officer pressed the button that changed the course of the cruiser.

The ship swung aside.

There was a rending crash as the rocky underside of the asteroid scraped the hull of the ship. The cruiser shuddered, righted herself.

The asteroid went past.

"I had to wait until it was almost too late." Vaston whispered. "If I shifted course too soon, the asteroid could have shifted to meet the new course. Now, it's going away." His eyes glittered.

A target that was going away was a target that even the poorest gunner could hit. Somewhere in the ship, an atomic cannon was being ranged and aimed. It fired—a single shot.

This time the shell struck home.

The empty ether of space shuddered under the impact of the explosion. From the core of this asteroid a mass of driving machinery spewed out. Again, flame beasts tried to flee from an atomic explosion.

Crane wiped sweat from his face, grinned at Vaston. "You're a topflight skipper, old man. You really did a swell job of handling that situation. Now for Ur-Gluk."

The Saturian fleet was coming up fast. The cruiser turned, took a deep breath, and bared her fangs again. She had fought, and fought again, and now she was as ready as utterly tired men could make her to fight another battle.

In the lead of the Saturian fleet was a big flier that was apparently the flagship. From its bow an explosion jutted.

"Firing at us!" Vaston nearly shouted. "They started this fight." His fingers moved to the firing button of the cruiser.

"Wait." Crane whispered.

OUTWARD from the Saturian fleet, the shell they had fired had exploded. It was not an atomic bomb; there was no mushroom of white smoke rolling out to the four corners of space.

It was a simple chemical shell, exploding in a shower of green skyrockets.

"That's a signal." Vaston said. "They're not firing at us, they're signaling to us."

"It's not possible," Crane breathed.

"Look for yourself. There are three green rockets. They came out of that shell. In the code of the Interplanetary Space Ship Rules, what do three green rockets mean?"

Crane knew what they meant. They spelled out these words:

DO YOU NEED HELP?

Three red skyrockets fired from a signal shell were a distress signal set up to be used by space ships whose radio equipment was out of order. Three green rockets constituted an offer of help.

Crane simply did not believe the evidence of his eyes. He sprang to the radio set, snapped the transmitter and receiver to the wave band assigned to Saturian vessels.

A voice was already coming in over the speaker.

"We wish to fight on the side of our human brothers. Tell us what to do."

It was the voice of Ur-Gluk, working through a communicator in the Saturian ship.

"Great God in Heaven." Crane breathed. "He is not only offering to help us but he is calling us brothers."

To him, this was a miracle almost beyond comprehension. The last time he had seen Ur-Gluk, the Saturian had been fighting his way through a door to escape from a flame beast.

Beside him, the girl whispered: "I told Ur-Gluk that what we wanted was peace and harmony. He has finally realized that it is best for all of us to work together."

Crane turned startled eyes toward her. In his mind was the thought that perhaps Trumbell had actually influenced the Saturian. But it would take more than the words of any human to make Ur-Gluk change his mind.

However, if Ur-Gluk was actually offering help, the only thing to do was to accept it. This was no time to worry about Saturian motives. Crane turned to the radio.

"We will point out an asteroid to you. Help us pursue it. Help us destroy it."

"Asteroid?" Even over the communicator in the Saturian ship and over the radio, the tone of Ur-Gluk's voice indicated that the Saturian was wondering if the human had taken leave of his senses. Everybody knew that asteroids were simply chunks of worthless rock. Why pursue one of them? Why try to destroy such a thing as an asteroid?

"It's the hiding place of the flame beasts," Crane said. "I don't know how they did it, but they exist inside asteroids. They have installed driving machinery of some kind—"

"The flame beasts!" Ur-Gluk's gasp was clear. "That's different. If they are concealed inside an asteroid, we will help our human brothers destroy it."

"Then go to work." Crane said grimly. He turned back to Vaston. The exec had already switched the view screen to the big asteroid.

"It's changed course." Vaston said. "And look...the flame beasts are leaving the ship."

THE SCREEN clearly revealed the flight of the flame creatures. Leaving off their circling of the cruiser, they were hurrying toward the asteroid, vanishing inside it. Whether they had given up the attempt to enter this perplexing cruiser, or whether some sudden call for them had gone out from the asteroid, was not known.

"Both the asteroid and the flame beasts are running!" Vaston shouted.

Swiftly, he changed the course of the ship, set it to follow the asteroid. Again the thud of the firing cannons came through the vessel.

Now it did not fight alone. Ranging beside it were the ships of the Saturian fleet.

To Johnson Crane, the knowledge that they did not fight alone was suddenly a very heady feeling. Ur-Gluk had meant his offer of help. Ur-Gluk was proving himself. The Saturian vessels were also firing on the asteroid. There was incontrovertible proof of Ur-Gluk's intentions.

Looking around him in the control room, Crane suddenly realized that he had had help from a thousand other sources too: from Vaston, sitting there in the control chair like a wooden-face image; from the technicians, from the radio operators, even from this girl. Down in the engine rooms was another man who had helped tremendously—Grimwald, the chief engineer.

The feeling came over him that he was not alone in this battle over Saturn, that he had never been alone. Always there had been others with him, working on the same problem.

"Look." Vaston whispered.

The view screen revealed shells striking the asteroid. It could take punishment, lots of it. It was so big, so tremendous, that even an atom bomb could not smash it.

But what one atomic explosion could not do, a dozen could. Suddenly, through some crevice or weak spot, a shell went home.

The explosion that took place out there under the rings of Saturn was a flaring column of mushrooming flame miles in extent. Inside the asteroid, some energy source used by the flame creatures had been ignited. The combination of the explosion from this energy source and the might of an atom bomb, created a flare of energy so vast and so tremendous that it was caught by alert astronomers back on Earth.

The explosion caught the cruiser, twisted and turned it. Vaston righted it. The impact also caught the vessels of the Saturian fleet. For several minutes there were wild maneuvers in space as the ships turned and twisted to dodge each other.

Then the ships were again in order.

Where the asteroid had exploded, only droplets of fading mist remained in the void.

"That's that," Crane said softly. "If there are any more of those flame beasts here inside the rings of Saturn, we will know how to deal with them."

"I wish to hell you'd tell me," Vaston said. "I've seen you make space suits radioactive, I've seen you use puffs of smoke to run those blasted ghosts lights out of the ship. I've had the idea that you were using radioactivity against them."

"And so I was," Crane answered. "Radioactivity is the one thing they can't stand. I don't know how or why it works this way, but radioactive energy is a deadly poison to them."

"All right," the dazed Vaston said. "But how did you discover they couldn't take radioactive particles?"

"When the first one appeared in the control room,

Captain Adams slapped at it with his arm. The creature ran from him. I saw the numerals of his wristwatch flare as he slapped at the creature. Those numerals were coated with luminous paint. The luminosity in this paint is actually a very mild form of radioactivity. When I leaped to help the man who was being devoured by the creature, I also slapped at it with the arm that held my wristwatch. Again the numerals flared. From that I made a wild guess."

"Whew!" was all the confounded Vaston said. But the look he gave Crane was one of the deepest admiration.

THE MEETING that took place later in the control room was historic in many ways. Admiral Harkness was there, wan and shaken. He made his report first. "We finally discovered that the only place on our ships where we were safe from the flame beasts was the engine rooms. We left the ships under automatic control and fled to the engine rooms for safety. Then, when the flame beasts left, we came out again."

"Good thinking," Crane said. The admiral looked relieved. "I intend to include a recommendation for you in my official report." The agent turned to Ur-Gluk.

The Saturian talked volubly over the communicator. "That flame beast almost destroyed our headquarters. I never saw such a scene of confusion in my life. When we finally managed to get rid of it, I made my decision instantly: that in the future I would fight on the side of my Earth brothers."

He looked defiantly at Crane as if he expected the human to deny him this privilege. Crane glanced sideways at Trumbell. She had thought that it was her argument for peace and harmony that had influenced. Ur-Gluk. Probably the Saturian had been influenced by what she had said but what had influenced Ur-Gluk far more was the flame beast. Ur-Gluk had actually been scared into cooperation. The girl, however, did not realize this fact. Crane grinned at Ur-Gluk.

"A very wise decision. I imagine you have given up all plans for a revolt."

A positive shudder passed over the Saturian. "But yes. But definitely."

Ur-Gluk spoke as if he meant every word he said. His manner indicated that if given time he would say a lot more words on this subject. Crane did not give him time. "How did you happen to come out into space to help us?"

"Our radar scanners reported a battle of some kind between Earth ships and the flame beasts was in progress. I promptly issued orders for my fleet to move to your aid. Planetary Government will no doubt accept my motives in this matter?"

"I cannot speak for Planetary Government but I am almost certain they will accept your change of heart. All they want is peace."

"Peace—that is what we Saturians want too." Ur-Gluk said firmly. Some of his nervousness left him. His color came up the scale to a healthy, shade of green.

"What about you?" Vaston spoke.

Crane shrugged. "I imagine Planetary Government will have some orders for me very soon."

IT WAS a shrewd guess. The orders came through. "Johnson Crane and Jane Trumbell will report to Earth at their convenience to make a fully detailed report of this situation."

The voice coming across space was that of a tired man reading an official order. Suddenly it lost a little of its tired feeling. A glow crept into it. "This is entirely unofficial, of course, but the idea seems to have gotten around here that perhaps you and Jane Trumbell would like to make your trip back to Earth part of a honeymoon—"

"Honeymoon." Crane almost gasped. The thought of

such a thing had never entered his mind. He couldn't believe what was happening. It was like the corny ending to an old-time movie.

The girl was speaking. "You heard what the man said. You didn't think you were going to get away from me without a honeymoon, did you?"

In her eyes was a glow and a sparkle, "Nor without this, either."

Her lips were close to his own. His face went down to meet them. Before the rather startled eyes of the assembled group, he kissed her.

Looking over the girl's shoulder, Crane saw that Ur-Gluk was watching him. Very gravely, he winked at Ur-Gluk. The Saturian looked startled. Crane sighed. The ways of the human race, in matters of love, would probably always be beyond the comprehension of a Saturian.

And sometimes, he thought, they were beyond the comprehension of a human too. He had not known he was in love with this girl. But she had known it. The instant she had mentioned it, he had realized that it was true.

With that knowledge, he was well content.

THE TALE is still told, out in the lanes of space, of the fire beasts that either evolved in the rings of Saturn, or came into that area from the vast gulf of space that lies beyond. In the limitlessness of space, there is room for all forms of life. The problem of the exact origin and the real nature of the flame beasts is as yet unsolved.

But sometimes when a meteor flames across a radar screen, lookouts on lonely freighters are a little startled, a little shivery, as they wonder if again they have met one of the flame beasts of the void.

THE END

HE HUNTED HORROR THROUGH A MANIAC WORLD!

Jeffery Meyer had killing on his mind—it was almost like a fever in his brain. It meant nothing to him that his towering Twenty-first Century world was going stark, staring mad. He shouldered aside the rising tide of narcotics-mania, the gambling fever, the insatiable lust for the irrational, because Jeff had his own all-consuming obsession—Paul Conroe must die!

After a five-year frenzied chase, Jeff had his victim cornered; he'd driven him into the last hideaway of the world's most desperate men—the sealed vaults of the human-vivisectionists. And Jeff knew that to reach his final horrible objective, he must offer himself as a guinea pig for the secret experiments of the world's most feared physicians!

CAST OF CHARACTERS

JEFF MEYER
Angry and obsessed with murder, he'd spent years tracking the man who killed his father. Finally, he had him cornered—sort of.

PAUL CONROE
A hunted and desperate man. Exactly how far would he go and what risks would he take to avoid his assassin?

DR. SCHIML
Lab animals wouldn't cut it anymore for this research scientist. He needed human volunteers—and their chances of survival were quite low.

BLACKIE
After volunteering as a "Medical Mercenary" she discovered an incredible power of mind locked in the recesses of her own brain.

THE NASTY FRENCHMAN
He'd waited a long time and taken great risks to get his turn for the "Big Cash". No one was going to stand in his way.

HARPO
His overpowering sense of greed drove him to participate in a murder conspiracy.

A MAN
OBSESSED

By
ALAN E. NOURSE

ARMCHAIR FICTION & MUSIC
PO Box 4369, Medford, Oregon 97504

CHAPTER ONE

JEFFREY MEYER sat back in his chair and waited. He could hardly breathe in the stifling air of the place. His hand clenched his glass until the knuckles were white, and his lip curled slightly as he watched the crowd around him. His whole body was tense. His legs, knotted tightly under the seat, were ready to move in an instant, and his eyes roved from the front to the back of the place. They were pale gray eyes that were never still—moving, watching, waiting. He had waited for so long, waited and hunted with bitter patience. But now he knew the long wait was drawing to a close. He knew that Conroe was coming and the trap was set.

For the thousandth time that evening, a shiver of chilly pleasure passed through him at the thought. He squirmed in eagerness, hardly daring to breathe. With his free hand he caressed the cool plastic handle of the gun that was close to his side, and a tight smile appeared on his thin lips. Conroe was coming...at last...at last... And tonight he would kill Conroe.

The place was a madhouse around him. In the front of the room, by the street door, was a long horseshoe bar. It was already crowded by the early revelers. A screechie in the corner blatted out the tinny, nervous music that had recently become so popular, and a loud, hysterical burst of feminine laughter echoed to the back of the room.

Jeff Meyer rubbed his eyes, smarting from the bluish haze filling the long, low-ceilinged room. The unhealthy laughter broke out again, and someone burst into a bellow of song, half giggle, half noise.

At the adjoining table an alky-siky stirred, muttered something unintelligible and returned his nose sadly to his glass. Jeff's eyes flicked over the man with distaste. The scrawny neck, the sagging jaw, the idiotic, almost unearthly expression of intent listening on the vapid face: a typical picture of the type. Jeff watched him for a moment in disgust, then moved his eyes on, still watching as a flicker of apprehension passed through his mind.

A girl, quite naked except for the tray slung at her waist, strolled by his table, wagging her hips and turning on her heaviest personality smile.

"Drive a nail, mister?"

"Beat it."

The smile cooled slightly on the girl's lips. "Just askin'," she whined. "You don't have to get—"

"Beat it!" Jeff shot her a venomous look, trying frantically to keep his attention from straying from the front of the room. It would be too much to slip up now, more than he could stand to make a mistake like the last time.

The trap was perfect. It *couldn't* fail this time. Each step of the way had been carefully sketched, plotted through long sleepless nights of conference and planning. They couldn't have hunted a man like Conroe all these years without learning something about him—about his personality, about the things he liked and disliked, the things he did, the places he frequented, the friends he made.

Last time, after Jeff's own blundering error had allowed him to slip through the net at the last frantic minute, there seemed to be no hope. Everything seemed all the more hopeless when the man had disappeared as completely as if he were dead. But then they had found the girl—the key to his hiding place. She had formed the top link in the long, meticulous chain which had been drawn tighter each day, drawing Paul Conroe at last closer and closer to the hands of the man who was going to kill him. And now the trap was set; there could be no slip this time. There might never be another chance.

The street door opened sharply, and a short, bull-necked man with sandy hair walked in. He was followed by two other men in neat business suits. The first man stepped quickly to the bar, shouldering his way through the crowd, and stood sipping beer for several minutes. He glanced closely at the people around the bar and the surrounding tables before he walked toward the back and seated himself next to Meyer. Looking at Jeff with an indefinable expression, he finished his beer at a gulp and set the glass down on the table top with a snap.

"What's up?" Jeff said hoarsely.

"Something's funny." The sandy-haired man's voice was a smooth bass, and a frown appeared on his pink forehead. "He should have been here by now. He left the hotel over in Camden-town an hour ago, private three-wheeler, and he headed for here."

Jeff leaned forward, his face going white. "You've got somebody on him?"

"Yes, yes, of course." The man's voice was sharp, and there were tired lines around his eyes. "Take it easy, Jeff. You wouldn't be able to get him if he did come in—the way you are. He'd spot you in two seconds."

Jeff's hand trembled as he gripped his glass, and he settled tensely back in his chair. "It can't go wrong, Ted. It's got to come off."

"It should. The girl is here and she got word from him last night."

"Can she be trusted?"

The sandy-haired man shrugged. "Don't be silly. In this game, nobody can be trusted. If she's scared enough, she'll play along—okay? We've done our best to scare her. We've scared the hell out of her. Maybe she's more scared of Conroe—I don't know. But it looks cold to me. On a platter. So get a grip on yourself."

"It's got to come off." Jeff growled the words savagely, and drained his glass at a gulp. The sandy-haired man blinked, his pale little eyes curious. He leaned back thoughtfully. "Suppose it doesn't, Jeff? Suppose something goes wrong? Then what?"

Jeff's heavy hand caught the man's wrist in a grip that was like a vise. "You don't talk like that," he grated. "Your men I don't mind, but not you—understand? It can't go wrong. That's all there is to it. No if's, no maybe's. You got that now?"

Ted rubbed his wrist, his face red. "All right," he muttered. "So it can't go wrong. So I shouldn't talk, I shouldn't ask questions. But if it does go wrong, you're going to be dead. Do you know that? Because you're killing yourself with this—" He sighed, staring at Meyer. "What's it worth, Jeff? This constant tearing yourself apart? You've been obsessed with it for years. I know, I've been working with you and watching you for the last five of them—five long years of hunting. And for what? To get a man and kill him. That's all. What's it worth?"

Jeff took a deep breath and took a pack of cigarettes from his jacket. "Drive a nail," he said, offering the pack. "And don't worry about me. Worry about Conroe. He's the one who'll be dead."

Ted shrugged and took the smoke. "Okay. But if this blows up, I'm through. Because this is all I can take."

"Nothing will blow up. I'll get him. If I don't get him now, I'll get him the next time, or the next, or the next. With or without you, I'll get him." Jeff took a trembling breath, his gray eyes cold under heavy black brows. "But there hadn't better be any next time."

He sat back in his chair, his face falling into the lines so familiar to Ted Bahr. Jeff Meyer had been a handsome man, before the long years of hate had done their work on his face.

He was a huge, powerfully built man, heavy-shouldered, with a strong neck and straight nose, and a shock of jet-black hair, neatly clipped. Only his face showed the bitterness of the past five years—years filled with anger and hatred, and a growing savagery which had driven the man almost to the breaking point.

The lines about his eyes and mouth were cruel—heavy lines that had been carved deeply and indelibly into the strong face, giving it a harsh, almost brutal cast in the dim light of the bistro. He breathed regularly and slowly as he sat, but his pale eyes were ice-hard as they moved slowly across the little show floor. They took in every face, every movement in the growing throng.

He was out of place and he knew it. He had no use for the giddy, half-hysterical people who crowded these smoke-filled holes night after night. They came in droves from the heart of the city to drink the watery gin and puff frantically on the contraband cigarettes as they tried desperately to drive off the steam and pressure of their daily lives.

Meyer hated the smell and stuffiness of the place; he hated the loud screams of laughter, the idiotic giggles; he hated the blubbering alky-sikys who crowded the bars with their whisky and their strange, unearthly dream worlds. Above all, he hated the horrible, resounding artificiality, the brassiness and clanging noise of the crowd. His skin crawled. He knew that he couldn't possibly disappear into such a crowd, that he was as obvious, sitting there, as if he had been painted with red polka dots. And he knew that if Conroe spotted him a second before he spotted Conroe— He eased back in the chair and fought for control of his trembling hands.

The lights dimmed suddenly and a huge red spotlight caught the curtain at the back of the show floor. Jeff heard Bahr catch his breath for a moment, then let out a small, uneasy sigh. The crowd hushed as the girl parted the curtains and stepped out onto the middle of the floor, to a fanfare of tinny music. Jeff's eyes widened as they followed her to the center of the red light.

"That's her."

Jeff glanced sharply at Bahr. "The girl? She's the one?"

Bahr nodded. "Conroe knows how to pick them. He's supposed to meet her later. This is her first show for the evening. Then she has another at ten and another at two. He's supposed to take her home." He glanced around the room carefully. "Watch yourself," he muttered, and silently slipped away from the table.

The girl was nervous. Jeff sat close enough to see the fear in her face as she whirled around the floor. The music had shifted into a slow throbbing undertone, as she started to dance. She moved slowly, circling the floor. Her hair was long and black, flowing around her shoulders, and her body moved with carefully calculated grace to the music. But there was fear in her face as she whirled, and her eyes sought the faces on the fringe of the circle.

The music quickened imperceptibly and Jeff felt a chill run up his spine. The upper part of the shimmering gown slipped from the girl's shoulders, and slowly the tempo of the dance began to change from the stately rhythm it had a moment before. The throb of the music became hypnotic, moving faster and faster. Jeff's hands trembled as he tried to draw his eyes away from the undulating figure. There had been nothing to mark the change, but suddenly the dance had become obscene as the music rose—so viciously obscene that Jeff nearly gagged.

He felt the tension in the crowd around him. He heard their breathing rise, felt the desperate eagerness in their hard, bright eyes as they watched. The nervousness had left the girl's face. She had forgotten her fear, and a little smile appeared on her face as her body moved in abandon to the quickening beat.

Slowly she moved toward the tables, and the spotlight followed her, playing tricks with her hair and gown, concealing and revealing, twisting and swaying... Jeff felt his body freeze. He fought to move, fought to take his eyes from the writhing figure as she drew closer and closer—

And then she was among the people, moving from table to table, never slowing her motion, graceful as a cat, twisting and twirling in the flickering red light. In and out she moved until she reached Jeff's table, her face inscrutable—a peacefully smiling mask. With amazing grace she leaped up on the tabletop and gave Jeff's glass a kick that sent it spinning onto the floor with a crash. And then the red light hit him full in the face—

"Get out of the light!"

Like a cat he threw his chair back and struck the girl, knocking her from the table. Someone screamed and the light swung to the girl, then back to him. The table went over. He rolled out of the light, twisting and fighting through the stunned and screaming crowd. His gun was in his hand, and he frantically searched the shouting room with his eyes.

"Get him! There he goes!"

He heard Bahr's voice roar from the side of the room. Jeff swung sharply to the sound of the voice. He saw the tall, slender figure crouched with his back to the bar, eyes wide with fear and desperation. There was no mistaking the face, the hollow cheeks and the high forehead, the graying hair. It was the face he had seen in his dreams, the twisted lips, the evil, ghoulish face of the man he had hunted to the ends of the earth. For a fraction of a second he saw Paul Conroe, crouched at bay, and then the figure was gone, twisting through the crowd toward the door—

"Stop him!" Jeff swung savagely into the crowd, screaming at Bahr across the room. "He's heading for the street! Get him!" The gun kicked sharply against his hand as he fired at the moving head. Rising for an instant, it disappeared again into the sea of heads. A scream rose at the shot. Women dropped to the floor, glasses crashed, tables went over. Someone clawed ineffectually for Jeff's leg. Then, abruptly, the lights went out and there was another scream.

"The door, the door—Don't let him get out—"

Jeff plunged to the side of the room, wrenched open the emergency exit and plunged down the dark, narrow walkway to the street. He heard shots as he ran. Turning the corner of the building, he saw the tall figure running pell-mell down the wet street.

"There he goes! Get him!"

Ted Bahr hung from the door. He gasped as he held his side, his face twisted in pain. "He hit me," he panted. "He's broken away—" A jet car slid from the curb and whined down the street toward the fleeing figure. "He can't make it—I've got men on every corner in cars. They'll get him, drive him back—"

"But where's he going?" A sob of rage choked Jeff's voice. "She sold us out, the bitch. She fingered me when she saw him come in—" His whole body trembled and the words tumbled out, almost incoherent. "But he must know the streets are blocked. Where's he running?"

"You think I'm a mind reader? I don't know. There are no open buildings in the whole block but this place and the Hoilman Center. He can't go anywhere else and he can't get out of the block. We've got every escapeway sewed up tight. He'll have to come back here or be shot down out there."

They watched the gloomy street, tears of rage in Jeff's eyes. His hands shook uncontrollably and his shoulders sagged in exhaustion and defeat. The tavern door had burst open and people were crowding out. Jeff and Ted Bahr moved back into the shadows of the alleyway and waited and listened.

"There's got to be a shot!" Jeff burst out. "He couldn't have slipped through." He turned to Bahr frantically. "Could he have gone into the Center?"

"On what pretense? They'd throw him to the Mercy Men—or the booby hatch, one or the other. He'd know better than to try." The sandy-haired man sank down on his haunches and gripped his side tightly. "He'll be back or we'll hear the shooting. He couldn't have slipped through."

A three-wheeled jet car slid in to the curb, and a man came up to them, eyes wide. "Get him?"

Bahr scowled. "No sign. How about the other boys?"

The man blinked. "Not a whisper. He never reached the end of the block."

"Did you check with Klett and Barker?"

"They haven't seen a soul down here."

Bahr glanced at Jeff sharply. "How about the streets behind? Any chance of a breakthrough there?"

The man's voice was matter-of-fact. "It's airtight. He couldn't get through without somebody seeing him." He stepped back to the car and spoke rapidly into the talker for a moment or two. "Nothing yet."

"Damn. How about Howie and the boys inside the place?"

"Nothing from them either."

Jeff's face darkened. "The Hoffman Center," he said slowly. "He got into the Center, somehow. He must have."

"He'd have to have gilt-edged medical credentials to get in after hours. They don't mess around over there. And what would it gain him?"

Jeff peered at Bahr in the darkness. "Maybe he wanted to be thrown to the Mercy Men. Maybe he's figured that as a last resort, he'll go in and volunteer, make a stab at the Big Cash."

Bahr stared at the big man in horror. "Look—Conroe may be desperate, but he hasn't lost his mind. My God, man! He isn't crazy."

"But he's scared."

"Of course he's scared, but—"

"How scared?"

Bahr shrugged angrily. "He'd have to be on his last legs to take a gamble like that."

"But they'd take him. They wouldn't ask any questions. They'd swallow him up; they'd hide him, whether they knew it or not." Jeff's voice rose in excitement. "Look. We've hunted him down for years. We've never rested; we've never quit. He knows that and he knows why. He knows me. He knows I'm not going to quit until I get him. And he knows I will get him, sooner or later. I'm cutting too close; I'm undermining his friends; I'm always moving closer. Everywhere he goes, everything he does, I'm onto him. And he knows when I do get him, he's going to die. What does that add up to?"

Bahr blinked in silence. Jeff's face hardened. "Well, I'll tell you what it adds up to. A man can take just so much. He can slide and twist and hide and keep moving just so long. Then he finds there aren't any more hiding places. But there's one last place a man can go to hide—if he's really at the end of his tether—and that's the Mercy Men. Because there he could vanish as though he'd never existed."

Ted Bahr carefully lit a smoke. "If that's where he went, we're through, Jeff. We'll never get him. We don't even need to worry about trying. Because if he's gone there, he'll never come out again."

"Some of them do."

Bahr grunted. "One in a million, maybe. The odds are so heavy that there's no sense thinking about it. If Paul Conroe has gone to the Mercy Men, then he's dead. And that is that."

Jeff returned his weapon to his pocket sharply and walked out to the car at the curb. "Keep your men where they are," he said to Bahr. "Keep them there for the rest of the night. If he's found a loophole, I want to know it. If he's hidden in the buildings, he'll have to come out sometime. Get some men to search the roofs, and you and I can start on the alleyways. If he's out there, we'll get him." He straightened his shoulders and the sullen fire was back in his eyes—an angry, bitter fire. "And if he's gone into the Center, we'll still get him."

Bahr's eyes were wide. "He'll never come out if he's gone where you think, Jeff. We could wait weeks or months, even years, and we still wouldn't know. Even if he did come out, we might never recognize him."

"I'll recognize him," Jeff snarled, looking down into Bahr's face. "I'm going to kill him. I'm going to know that he's dead, because I'll see him die. And I'll kill him if I have to follow him into the Center to do it."

CHAPTER TWO

THE NEWS report blatted in Jeff Meyer's ear from the little car radio. The words came through, but he hardly heard them as his eyes watched the huge glass doors of the administration building of the Hoffman Medical Center.

...no word has yet been received, but it is believed that the Eurasian governments may be in session several hours more in an attempt to stem the inflation. On the home front, the stock-market nosedive, which resulted from the new Senate taxation bill yesterday, leveled off when the Secretary of Corporative Business announced this morning that the government would abandon attempts to enforce the new law, at least for the time being. Secretary Barnes stated that further study of the bill would be undertaken when more pressing governmental problems had been cleared—

Jeff snapped off the switch with a snarl. The street passing the Center was crowded. Lines of cars moved into and out of the traffic stream from the huge Center parking tiers. The building rose high, tier upon tier. Its walls gleamed white in the bright morning sunlight, reflecting brilliant facets of golden light from thousands of polished windows.

It was an immense building, sprawling across six perfectly landscaped city blocks, tall trees and cool green terraces setting off the glistening beauty of the architecture. The structure sent tower after tower up from the dingy street below, and at the foot of the towers was a buzz of furious activity. Supply trucks, carrying food and supplies for the twenty-two thousand beds and the people in them, and for the additional thirteen thousand people who worked day and night to keep the huge hospital running, moved toward the unloading platforms.

The Hoffman Medical Center was an age-old dream that had finally come true. Even those who had conceived it had not realized the tremendous need it would fulfill. From its very inception, no expense had been spared. The finest architects had thrown up the shimmering ward-towers, turned toward the sun, to bring light to the sick and injured who rested and healed within. Equipment unequaled anywhere in the world had filled the Center's dressing and surgical rooms. The doctors, nurses, researchers and technicians who staffed the institution had been gathered from the world over. And all the world had conceded the Hoffman Center its place as leader in the realm of medicine, ever since the cornerstone had been laid that rainy morning in the spring of the year 2085. Twenty-four years had passed since that day, and in those years the Hoffman Center had never once faltered in its leadership.

The men in the car sat in stony silence. Finally, Jeff Meyer stirred, extended his hand briefly to Ted Bahr. "You'll cover things out here?"

"Don't worry about it." Bahr shook the hand. "We'll wait to hear from you." He watched, almost wistfully, as the huge man cut through the traffic and headed for the large glass doors. Then, with a sigh, he stepped on the starter button and snaked the little jet car into the stream of traffic moving toward the city.

Jeff Meyer stopped in the great, bustling lobby and stared about him almost in awe. He had never been inside the Hoffman Center before, though he had heard of it many times and in many places. Since it had taken over service of the huge metropolis of Boston-New Haven-New York--Philadelphia, the newspapers and TV had been full of stories of the lifesaving and healing that had gone on within its walls. The disease research, conducted by specialists in all phases of medicine who were for the first time gathered together under one agency, had startled the world again and again.

But there had been other stories, too—not from the papers and TV, not these stories. These tales had come by word of mouth: a short sentence or two, a nervous laugh, a sneering joke, a rumor, a whispered story from a wide-eyed alky hanging over a bar. Not the sort of stories one really believed, but the sort that made one wonder.

Several dozen white-garbed women moved across the floor of the huge lobby and talked quietly among themselves. Jeff sniffed uneasily. There was a curiously distasteful odor in the air, an odor of almost unhealthy cleanliness and spotless preservation. The lobby was a mill of activity: the elevators and interbuilding jitneys terminated here; people moved briskly, carrying with them the familiar air of hurry and vast pressure that infected the whole world outside.

Jeff watched, spotting the corridor leading to the main administrative offices. He saw the elevators constantly rising to and returning from the huge admission offices. He noted the corridor twisting off to the staff living quarters. He stood silent, his quick gray eyes cautiously probing and watching. He tried to print an indelible picture in his mind of the layout of the building and was almost floored by the hive-like bustle of the place. There was a complexity in the curved doorways and the brightly-lighted corridors.

Somewhere here he could find Paul Conroe. Somewhere in this maze of buildings and passageways was the man he had hunted for. Logic told him that. They had spent the night searching every possible alternative. His muscles ached and his eyes were red from sleeplessness, but there was a hot, angry glow in his heart. He knew that this was the only place that Conroe could have gone. Yet the place where he must be hiding was a place Jeff had heard of only in rumor, a place whose mention carried with it a half-knowledge of staggering wealth and almost indescribable horror.

Someone tapped him on the shoulder. He turned, startled, to face a huge, burly man with a suspicious face and a gray uniform. "You got business here, mister, or are we just sightseeing?"

Jeff forced a grin. "I don't know where to go," he said truthfully.

"Maybe you should go back out then. No visitors until this afternoon."

"No, I'm not a visitor. I'm looking for the Volunteer's Bank. The ads said to come to the administration offices—"

The guard's face softened a little. He pointed a finger toward a corridor marked RESEARCH ADMINISTRATION. "Right over there," he said. "Office is the first door to your right. The nurse will take care of you."

Meyer strolled toward the corridor, his mind fumbling with the rumors and bits of half-knowledge that were all that he had to work on: stories of drunks stumbling into the Emergency Rooms and never coming out; tales of quiet, swift raids on narcotics houses, of people who never reached the police stations.

But how could he make the right contact here? "Research Administration" covered a multitude of meanings. He had read the advertisements for Hoffman volunteers in all the buses, in the 'copters, on the roads. Newspapers and TV had carried them for years. Meyer glanced down at his un-polished shoes, rubbed a finger over his purposely unshaven chin. What would they expect a volunteer to look like? How could they detect a fraud, an interloper? He shivered as he faced the office door. It would be a gamble, a terrible chance. Because with all the other publicity, no mention had ever been made of the Mercy Men. He glanced back, found the guard still staring at him, and walked into the office.

Several people sat along the wall. A small, mousy-looking man with a baldhead and close-set eyes had just sat down in the chair before the desk. He waited for the prim-looking woman wearing a ridiculous little white hat to put down her pen. She didn't even glance up as Jeff took a seat, and she kept writing for several minutes before turning her attention to the little bald man. Then she looked up and gave a frosty smile at him. "Yes, sir?"

"Dr. Bennet asked me to come back today," the little man said. "Follow-up on last week's work."

"Name please?" The woman took his name and punched the button on a panel before her; an instant later a card flipped down in a slot. She checked it, made an entry and nodded to the man. "Dr. Bennet will be ready for you at eleven. You'll find magazines in the lounge." She indicated another door, and the little man disappeared through it.

Another person, a middle-aged woman, moved to take the little man's place before the desk. Jeff felt restless and glanced at his watch. It was almost eleven. Must she move so slowly? Nothing seemed to hurry her. She worked from person to person, smiling, impersonal, just a trifle chilly. Finally she nodded to Jeff, and he moved to the chair.

"Name, please?"

"You don't have a card on me."

She looked up briefly, "A new volunteer? We're happy to have you, sir. Now if you'll give me your name, I can start the papers through."

Jeff cleared his throat, felt his pulse pounding in his forehead. "I'm not sure just what I want to volunteer for," he said cautiously.

The woman smiled. "We have a rather large selection to choose from. There are the regular 'mycin drug runs every week on Tuesdays and Thursdays. You take the drug by mouth in the morning and give blood samples at ten, two and four. Many of our new Volunteers start on that. It pays six dollars and your lunch while you're here. Or you could give blood, but the law restricts you to once every three months on that, and it only pays thirty-five dollars. Or—"

Jeff shook his head and leaned forward. He looked directly into her eyes. "I don't think you understand," he said softly. "I want money. Lots of it. Not five or ten dollars." He looked down at the desk. "I've heard you have other kinds of work."

The woman's eyes narrowed. "There are higher-paying categories of Volunteer work, of course. But you must understand that they are higher paying because they involve a greater risk to the health of the Volunteer. For instance, we've been running circulation studies with heart catheterizations. We pay a hundred dollars for these, but there is an appreciable risk involved. Or sternal marrow punctures for blood studies. Usually we start—"

"I said money," said Jeff implacably. "Not peanuts."

Her eyes widened and she stared at him for a long moment. It was a strange, penetrating stare that took him in from his face to his feet. Her smile faded and her fingers were suddenly nervous. "Have you any idea what you're talking about?"

"I have. I'm talking about the Mercy Men."

She stood up abruptly and disappeared into an inner office. Jeff waited, his whole body trembling. Beads of sweat broke out on his forehead, and he gave a visible start when the woman opened the door again.

"Come in here, please."

Then he was on the right track. He tried to conceal the excitement in his eyes as he took a seat in the small room. He waited, fidgeting. The woman picked up a small telephone on the desk and punched several buttons in rapid succession. The silence was almost intolerable as he waited, a silence that was alive and vibrant. Finally a signal light flickered and she took up the receiver.

"Dr. Schiml? This is the Volunteer office, Doctor." She shot Jeff a swift glance. "There's another man here to see you."

Meyer felt his heart pound. He shifted in his chair and started to take out a cigarette. Then he checked himself.

"That's right," the woman was saying, eyeing him as if he were a biological specimen. "I'm sorry, he hasn't given a name... Ten minutes? All right, Doctor, I'll have him wait." With that, she replaced the receiver and left the room without a word.

Jeff stood up, stretched his legs and looked about the room. It was small, with just a desk and two or three chairs. Obviously it served as a conference room of some sort. One wall held the panel of file buttons; another held the telephone and visiphone viewer. Over the visiphone screen, a large lighted panel announced the date in sharp black letters: 32 April, 2109. Below it, the little transistor clock had just changed to read 11:23 A.M. Almost noon. And every passing minute his quarry drew farther and farther away.

He glanced out the window at the rising tiers of buildings. Across the courtyard the first of the ward-towers rose. To one side of it were a series of long, low structures with skylights. These were the kitchens, perhaps, or maintenance buildings. There were dozens of them—anyone of which could be hiding Paul Conroe. Jeff clenched his hands until the nails bit his palms. He stared down at the buildings. Conroe could be anywhere down there. *Another man had already seen Dr. Schiml...*

A door clicked behind him and he turned sharply. A man entered the room and closed the door behind him. Smiling, he walked over to the desk. Meyer nodded and watched the man. He felt a sinking feeling in the pit of his stomach. For the briefest instant the doctor had caught his eye, and Jeff felt everything that he had planned to say crumble like dust around him.

The man hardly looked like a doctor, although his white jacket was immaculate and a stethoscope peeped from his side pocket. He was tall and slender, almost fifty years old, with round, cheerful pink cheeks and a little pug nose that seemed completely out of place on his face.

A harmless-looking man, Jeff thought, except for his eyes. But his eyes—they were the sharpest, most penetrating eyes Jeff had ever seen. And they were watching him. Quite independent of the smiling face, they watched his every move, studying him. The eyes were full of wisdom, but they were also tinged with caution.

The doctor sat down and motioned Jeff to the seat facing

the desk. He pushed a cigar case across the desk to him.

Jeff hesitated, then took one. "I thought these were slightly illegal," he said.

The doctor grinned. "Slightly. Thanks to us, as you probably know. We did most of the work here on tobacco smoke and cancer—actually got legislation pushed through on it." He leaned back easily in his chair as he lit his own cigar. "Still, one once in a while won't do too much harm. And there's nothing like a good smoke to get things talked out. I'm Roger Schiml, by the way. I didn't get your name."

"Meyer," said Jeff. "Jeffrey Meyer."

The doctor's eyes narrowed quizzically. "I hope my girl didn't bother you too much. She channels most of the volunteer work here, as you see. Then, occasionally, cases come in which she'd rather turn over to me." He paused for a moment. "Cases like yours, for instance."

Jeff blinked, his mind racing. It would take acting, he thought, real acting to fool this man. The face was deceptively young and benign, almost complacent. But the eyes were far from young. They were old, old eyes. They had seen more than eyes should see. They missed nothing. To fool a man with eyes like that— Jeff took a deep breath and said, "I want to join the Mercy Men."

Dr. Schiml's eyes widened very slightly. For a long moment he said nothing, just stared at the huge man before him. Then he said, "That's interesting. It's also very curious. The name, I mean—oh, I can understand the attraction such an idea might have for people, but the name that's become so popular—it baffles me. 'Mercy Men.' It gives you a curious feeling, don't you think? Brings up mental pictures of handsome young interns fighting the forces of evil and death, the brave heroes giving their all for the upward flight of humanity—all that garbage, you know." The eyes hardened quite suddenly. "Where did you hear of the Mercy Men, I wonder?"

Jeff shrugged. "The word's been around for quite a while. A snatch here, a story there—even though it isn't advertised too openly."

Dr. Schiml looked him straight in the eye. "And suppose I told you that there is no such organization, either here or anywhere else on Earth that I know of?"

A tight smile appeared on Jeff's face. "I'd call you a class-A liar."

Schiml's eyebrows went up. "I see. That's a big word. Maybe you can support it."

"I can. There are Mercy Men here. There have been for several years."

"You're sure of that."

"Quite. I know one. He was a skid-rower with a taste for morphine when I first ran into him—a champagne appetite to go with a beer income. Then he went out of circulation for about six months. Now he has a place up in the Catskills, with many, many thousands of dollars in the bank. Of course, he uses the money to feed several hundred cats in his basement." Jeff's eyes narrowed. "He never liked cats very much before he left here. There are other funny things he does—nothing serious, of course, but peculiar. Still, he doesn't need the dope any more."

Schiml smiled and put his fingers together. "That would be Luke Tandy. Yes, Luke was a little different when he left, but the work was satisfactory and we paid off."

"Yes," said Jeff softly. "One hundred and fifty thousand dollars. Cash on the line. To him or his heirs. He was lucky."

"So what are you doing here?"

"I want a hundred and fifty thousand dollars too."

The doctor's eyes met Jeff's squarely. "And you are a liar too."

Jeff reddened. "What do you mean—"

"Look, let's get this straight right now. Don't lie to me. I'll catch you every time." The doctor's eyes were hard. "I see a man who's eaten well for a long time, wearing dirty but expensive clothes, who doesn't drink, who doesn't use drugs, who is young and strong and capable. He tells me he wants to join the Mercy Men for money. He tells me a lie. Now I'll ask you again: why are you here?"

"For money. For one hundred and fifty thousand dollars." The doctor sighed and leaned back. "All right, no matter. We'll go into it later, I suppose. But I think you'd better understand certain things. It's no accident that your information on the Mercy Men is so vague. We've been careful to keep it that way, of course. The more vague the stories, the fewer curiosity-seekers and busybodies we have to contend with. Also, the more distasteful the stories, the more desperate people will become before they come to us. This we particularly desire. Because the work we do here requires a very desperate man to volunteer."

As he talked, the doctor brought out a pack of cards from the desk and began riffling them nervously in his fingers. Jeff's eyes caught them and a chill went down his back. They were curious cards, not the regular playing variety. These were smaller, with a peculiar marking system in bright red on the white faces. Jeff shivered and he was puzzled at the chill that gripped his body. He shifted in his chair in growing tension and tried to take his eyes from the cards.

The doctor snubbed out his cigar, leaned back in the chair and gave the cards a riffle and regarded Jeff closely. "We've done a lot here since the Center opened—work based on years of background research. A century or more ago there were terrible medical problems to be faced: polio was a killer then; they had no idea of cancer control; they were faced with a terrific death rate from heart disease. All those things are beaten now, a thing of the past. But as the old killers moved out, new ones took their place. Look at the half-dozen NVI plagues we've had in the past few years—neurotoxic virus infections that started to appear out of nowhere twenty years ago. Look at the alky-sikies you see in every bar today, a completely new type of alcoholism-psychosis that we haven't even been able to describe, much less cure. Look at the statistics on mental disease, rising in geometric progression almost every year."

The tall doctor stood up and walked to the window. "We don't know why it's happening, but it is. Something's on the march, something ghastly and evil among the people. Something that has to be stopped." He gave the cards a sharp riffle and tossed them onto the desk with a sigh. "We can't stop it until we know something about the human brain and how it works, and why it does what it does, and how. We don't even understand fully the structure of the nervous system, much less understand its function. And we've learned all we can from cats and dogs and monkeys. Any further study of a monkey's brain will give us great insight into the neuroses and complexes of monkeys, no doubt. But it won't teach us anything more about men." His voice was very soft. "You can see where this leads, I think."

Jeff Meyer nodded slowly. "You need men," he said.

"We need men. Men to study. Cruel as it may sound, men to experiment upon. We can't learn any more from any other variety of...experimental animal. But there are problems. Toy around with a man's brain and he is likely to die, quite abruptly. Or he may be deranged, or he may go violently insane. Most of the work, however well planned, however certain we were of results, however safe it appeared, proved to be completely unpredictable. Much of the work and many of the results were quite horrible. But we're making progress, slow—but progress nonetheless. So the work continues.

"It hasn't been very popular. No man in his right mind would volunteer for such a job. So we hired men. For the most truly altruistic work in the world, our workers come with the most mercenary of motives: we pay for their services and we pay well. A hundred thousand dollars is a small fee, on our scale. We have the government behind us. The sky is the limit, if we need a man for a job. The money is paid, when the work is completed, either to the man himself or to his heirs. You see why the name they've given themselves is so curious—Medical Mercenaries, the 'Mercy Men.' That's why a man must be desperate to come to us. That's why we must be so very careful who joins us, for what motives."

Jeff Meyer stared at his hands and waited in the silence of the room. His eyes strayed once again to the curious cards, and the chill of fear went through him like a ghastly breeze. This was a port of last resort, a road that could end in horror and death. Ted Bahr had said it wasn't worth it, that Conroe would never escape alive—but he knew that Conroe could. And he knew Conroe well enough to know that he would.

Jeff felt the old bitterness and hatred swell up in his mind, and his hands trembled as he sat. He had long since thrown aside his life as he had known it, cast off the veneer of civilized life that he had acquired, to hunt Paul Conroe down and kill him. There was nothing else in his life that mattered. It had been a long, grueling hunt, tracking him, following him, studying him, tracing his movements and habits, plotting trap after trap, driving the man to desperation. But there had been no indication, anywhere along the line that Conroe would turn to such a desperate gamble as this.

But he must have known that death otherwise was inevitable. Here he could be changed. He might disappear from the face of the Earth in the oblivion of quiet death, to be sure, but he also might emerge, unscathed, to live in wealth the rest of his life, unrecognizable and safe.

Jeff Meyer looked up at the doctor and his eyes were hard. "I haven't changed my mind," he said. "What has to be done to join?"

Dr. Schiml sighed, and turned resignedly to the file panel. "There are tests that are necessary and rules to be obeyed. You'll be confined and regimented. And once you're assigned to a job and sign a release, you're in." He leaned forward and punched the visiphone button. Tapping his fingers idly on the desk, he waited until an image blinked and cleared on the screen. "Blackie," he said tiredly. "Better send the Nasty Frenchman up here. We've got a new recruit."

The visiphone snapped off and Jeff sat frozen to his seat, his pulse throbbing in his neck, every nerve in his body screaming in excitement. The face on the screen had been clearly visible for a moment: a pale face with large gray eyes—a woman's face, surrounded by flowing black hair. It was a face that was impressed indelibly on his memory. It belonged to the girl who had danced the night before in the red light.

CHAPTER THREE

THERE was no doubt of it. She was the girl in the night club, the dancing girl with the flowing black hair and the mask-like smile, who had led him to Conroe and then brought the spotlight to his face to spring the trap too soon. Frantically Jeff fought to control his excitement. He knew his face was white and he avoided the doctor's puzzled glance. But he couldn't control the angry fire burning in his mind, the little voice screaming out: *"He's here; he's here, somewhere!"*

But why was she here? The doctor had called her "Blackie." He had spoken to her with familiarity. Jeff's mind whirled. He had the strangest feeling that he had missed something somewhere along the line that he knew the answer but couldn't quite grasp it. What could the girl's sudden appearance in the Center involve?

Or had her appearance at the nightclub been the unusual one?

A buzzer rang and the office door opened to admit a small, weasel-faced man. The doctor looked up and smiled. "Hello, Jacques. This is Jeff Meyer, the new recruit. Take him down and get him quartered in, all right? And you might brief him a little. He's awfully green."

The little man scratched his long nose and regarded Jeff with a nasty smile. "A new one, huh? Where are you going to line him up?"

"No telling. We'll see where the tests put him, first. Then we'll talk about jobs."

The smile widened on the little man's face, turning down the end of his long pointed nose and revealing a dirty yellow row of teeth. His eyes ran over Jeff from head to toe. "Big one too. But then, they fall just as hard as the rest. Want me to take him right down?"

Schiml nodded. "Maybe he can still get lunch." His eyes shifted to Jeff. "This is the Nasty Frenchman," he said, motioning toward the little man with his thumb. "He's been around for a long time; he can show you the ropes. And don't let him bother you too much—his sense of humor, I mean. Like I say, he's been around here a long time. You'll get quarters and you'll be expected to stay with your group for meals and everything else. That means no contacts outside the hospital as long as you're here. You'll get the daily news reports, and there are magazines and books in the library. If you've got other business outside, you haven't any business in here. Any time you leave the Center it's considered an automatic breach of contract."

He paused for a long moment and gave Jeff a strange look, almost a half smile. "And you'll find that questions aren't appreciated around here, Jeff. Any kind of questions. The men don't like people too much when they ask questions."

The Nasty Frenchman shuffled his feet nervously, and Jeff started out the door. Then the little man turned back to Dr. Schiml. "They brought Tinker back from the table about ten minutes ago. He's in pretty bad shape. Maybe you should look at him?"

"This was the big job today, wasn't it?" Schiml's eyes were sharp. "What did Dr. Bartel say?"

"He said no dice. It was a bust."

"I see. Well, it may be just the diodrax wearing off now, but I'll be down to see."

The Nasty Frenchman grunted and turned back to Jeff.

His face still wore the nasty little grin. "Let's go, big boy," he said, and started down the hall.

Jeff watched the corridors as they passed, counting them one by one, trying desperately to keep himself oriented. He glanced at his watch and angrily sucked in his breath. Minutes were slipping by, precious minutes, minutes that could mean success or failure. A thousand questions crowded his mind, and behind them all was the girl. She was the key, he was sure of it. She would know where Conroe was, where he could be found...

They reached an elevator, stepped aboard and shot down at such dizzying speed that Jeff nearly choked. Then, suddenly, they came to a jolting stop and stepped into a dingy, gray corridor that was dimly lit by bare bulbs in the ceiling.

The Nasty Frenchman punched a button in the wall and turned to regard Jeff. The sneering little smile was still on his lips as the far-off rumble of a jitney grew to a sharp clatter. A little car dropped down from its ceiling track. The little man hopped in nimbly and motioned Jeff in beside him. Then the car took off for the ceiling again, swinging crazily and speeding down the maze of corridors and curves.

Jeff stirred uneasily, growing more and more confused with every turn. "Look," he broke out finally, "where's this thing taking us?"

The Nasty Frenchman turned pale eyes toward him. "You worried or something?"

"Well, it looks like we're headed for the center of the Earth. I'd like to be able to find my way out sometime—"

"Why?"

The question was so blunt that it left Jeff's jaw sagging for a moment. "Well, I'm not planning to spend the rest of my life in here."

The Nasty Frenchman guffawed. It was not a pleasant laugh. "Here for a nice restful vacation, huh? You wise guys are all the same. Go ahead, dream—I won't bother you."

The little man turned his attention to the controls and the car swung sharply to the right and headed down another corridor. Jeff scowled as he watched the lighted corridors flash by. Were they speeding so far, so deep in the depths of the building? Or was this part of a definite plan to confuse, to lose recruits in the mammoth place so completely that they could never find their way out? Jeff shrugged, finally. It really didn't matter too much. He had one job and only one. He could worry about escape when it had been accomplished.

"That girl," he said finally. "The doctor called her 'Blackie.' Is she down here where we're going?"

"How should I know? I don't keep her on a leash." The little man's face darkened and his eyes turned suspiciously to Jeff.

"I mean, is she one of the group—one of the Mercy Men?"

The Nasty Frenchman threw a switch sharply, swerving

the speeding car through a long, dim passage. He ignored the question, as if he hadn't heard it. In the dim light his skin was pasty yellow and wrinkled like a mummy. The cruelty and avarice on his face was frightening.

Jeff watched him for a moment or two, then said, "What brought you here? To the Mercy Men, I mean?"

The Nasty Frenchman's eyes flashed poisonously, his face a horrid mask. "Did I ask you your racket before you came in?"

"No."

"Then don't ask me mine. And you won't forget that, if you're smart." He turned his attention sharply to the controls, ignoring Jeff for several moments. Finally he said, "You'll share a room and you'll eat at eight, noon and six. Tests should start tomorrow morning at eight-thirty. You'll be in your room when the doctors come for you. You won't have any status here until you're tested. Then you'll sign a release and wait for a job assignment. You won't have any choice of work; that's just for the older ones. Some of the work is with central nervous system, some is with sympathetic; some work concentrates on spinal cord and peripherals, but most of the interest these days is in cortical lesions and repair. That pays the best, too—couple hundred thousand at a crack, with a fairly good risk."

"And what's a fairly good risk in here?"

The grin reappeared on the little man's face again. It was almost savage in its cruelty. "Ten per cent full recovery is a good risk. That means complete recovery from the work, no secondary infection, complete recovery of faculties—in other words complete success in the work. Then a fairly good risk runs slightly lower—more casualty, maybe five per cent recovery. And a high-risk job averages two per cent—"

The grin broadened. "You've got a better chance of living sitting under an atom bomb, my friend. And once you sign a

release, relieving the hospital and the doctors of all re-
sponsibility, you're in, and held to your contract by law. This
is no vacation, but if you're lucky enough to come through—
" The little man's eyes were bright with eagerness. "They pay
off—oh, how they payoff. If you're lucky, you'll get a good
starter, maybe a hundred thousand, with good risk."   He
scratched his nose and regarded Jeff closely.   "Of course,
there are incomplete recoveries, too.   They have trouble
keeping them out of the news, if they ever leave.   Pretty
messy, sometimes, too."

Jeff felt his face paling at the cruel eagerness in the little
man's voice. What could bring a man to a place like this—
especially this kind of a man?   Or had he been a different
kind of a man before he came in?   How long had he been
here, waiting from experiment to experiment, waiting to live
or to die, waiting for the payoff, the Big Cash that waited at
the end of a job? What could such an existence do to a man?
What could there be to drive him on? Jeff shuddered, then
gasped as the car gave a sudden lurch around a corner and
settled to the floor.

The Nasty Frenchman hopped out, motioned to Jeff to
follow. They started walking toward the escalator at the end
of the passageway. Jeff searched each doorway they passed,
keeping alert for a sign of the black-haired woman. "Look,"
he said finally. "This girl—Blackie, I mean—who is she?"

The Nasty Frenchman stopped in his tracks, glared at Jeff.
"What is she, an old family friend or something? You keep
asking about her."

"I know her from somewhere."

"So why bother me with your questions?"

Jeff's face darkened angrily. "I want to see her, all right?
Don't get so jumpy—"

The little man whirled on him like a cat. Jeff's arm was
wrenched behind his back until he felt the tendons rip. With

unbelievable strength the Nasty Frenchman twisted the huge man back against the wall and glared up at him with blazing eyes. "You're a smart guy, coming around here, asking questions," he snarled, giving Jeff's arm a vicious wrench. "You think you can fool me? You ask about this, you ask about that—why so nosey? Blackie...me...everything. What are you doing here? Going after the Big Cash or asking questions?"

"The Cash!" Jeff gasped. He twisted to wriggle free of the iron-like grip.

"Then don't ask questions! We don't like nosey people here; we like people that roll dice square and mind their own business." The little man gave the arm a final agonizing wrench and released it. He jumped back, poised, eyes savagely eager.

Every instinct screamed at Jeff to rush him, but he slumped against the wall. Rubbing his aching arm, he fought for control. He knew a fight now could ruin things completely. Already he had blundered terribly. He cursed under his breath. How stupid he'd been not to have realized how unpopular questions would be to people in a place like this. And surely the word would get to the girl now that he was asking about her. Unless he could get to her first—

Still rubbing his elbows painfully, he turned to the Nasty Frenchman. "Okay, let it go," he growled. "Where do we go from here?"

The room was small and barren. Dingy and gray, it matched Jeff's spirit perfectly. He entered it with the Nasty Frenchman at his heels and stared at the two stark hospital beds against the far wall, the two foot lockers, the two small desk-and-chair combinations. There was no window in the room. Indeed, there was nothing about the room or corridor to prove that they were not twenty miles underground. Certainly the jitney ride had been no reassurance to the contrary.

The dim wall lights glowed on scrubbed, peeling paint, and the floor was covered with clean but well-worn plastic matting. Against one wall was a TV set. Between the beds a door led into a compact lavatory and shower. Glancing in, Jeff saw the lavatory was also connected with the adjoining room.

"It's no Grand Hotel," the Nasty Frenchman said sourly. "But it's clean and it's a bed. This corridor quarters your whole unit—the C unit. Other units are on other floors, up and down."

Jeff looked around the room gloomily. "Where can I eat?"

"The mess hall's four flights down. Take the escalator at the end of the hall. It closes in half an hour, so you'd better step on it. And if you're smart, you won't go wandering around. These boys in gray you see here and there don't like us very much." His face creased into a sardonic grin as he started for the door. "And you'd be smart to change before you come down. The faster people stop thinking you're new here, the happier you'll be." With that, he turned and disappeared down the hall.

Jeff gave a sigh, and prowled the room. One of the footlockers held an amazing assortment of clean and dirty clothes. On the floor of it lay a large heap of dirty shirts and trousers, and nested squarely in the center of the pile was a heap of gold rings and wristwatches. Jeff blinked, not quite believing his eyes. He hadn't thought to ask about his room-mate, but apparently he had one who had not yet made his appearance.

Apparently everyone wore similar clothing. He found the other locker filled with clean shirts and dungarees. Swiftly he started to change, his mind racing. His body was sore all over and he felt a dry, hot feeling around his ears from lack of sleep. His arm ached miserably every time he moved it. If only he could sleep for a little while. But he knew there was no time to be wasted. In the mess hall there would still be people. Somewhere among them he would find the girl...

Carefully he considered the problem. The girl was the key. He had to find her, to make certain that Conroe was here. And he had to find her quickly, catch her unawares, before she had a chance to alibi or hide. Conroe would be hidden; he would never come into the open until he was sure that he had not been followed. He too must be taken unawares. Jeff had seen Conroe slip out of too many traps in the past. A blunder now could be the last. And if Conroe had time to plan, there would be many, many blunders.

A car buzzed down the hall as he stood in the room and stopped a little way from the door. There were voices, subdued, yet carrying a sharp note of frantic excitement. Jeff paused, listening to the combination of unfamiliar sounds: a grunt, a low curse, a rustle of whispered conversation, a low whistle. Then the door to the next room banged open and a rumble and squeak of wheels came to his ears.

"Jeez, what a job!"

"Yeah, looks bad. Did the doc see him?"

"He said he'd be down—"

"—gotta let it wear off before you can tell. This was the works, this time."

Jeff walked quietly to the door of the connecting lavatory, his nerves tingling. A new sound was apparent, an unearthly sound of labored, gurgling breathing. Jeff shivered. He had heard a sound like that only once before in his life: in a rocket during the Asian war, when a man had been struck in the throat with a chunk of shrapnel. Carefully, he pushed the door open an inch, peered through...

There were three men standing in the room, maneuvering a man—if it was a man—from the four-wheeled cart onto the bed. The man's head was covered to the shoulders with bandage. A patch of fresh blood showed near the temple, and a rubber tube emerged where the mouth should have been.

"Got him down? Better cover him closer. Restrainers—he may jump around. Doc said three weeks for shock to wear off, if he makes it through the night."

"Yeah—and this is the Big Cash for Tinker too. Harpo nearly beat him to the job, but Schiml had promised him—"

Jeff shuddered. This, then, was one of the Mercy Men, finished with a "job." The gurgling sound grew louder, measuring itself with the man's breathing—short, shallow, a measure of death. An experiment had been completed.

Jeff closed the door silently. His face in the mirror was pasty white and his hands were shaking. Here was the factor that had been plaguing him from the start, finally breaking through to the surface. The road he was traveling was a one-way road. He had to find Conroe and get off the road quickly, while he could. *Because he dared not travel the road too far.*

The air in the corridor seemed fresher as Jeff started for the escalator. It was almost two o'clock and he hurried, anxious to reach the mess hall before it closed. He consciously fought the picture of the man on the bed out of his mind. With effort he focused his attention once again on the girl. At the end of the corridor he stepped onto the creaky, down-going escalator.

If only he could check with Ted Bahr, make certain that the trail had really ended at the Hoffman Center, make sure that Conroe was not really somewhere outside, still hiding, still running. One thing seemed certain: if Conroe were really here, he too would be faced with the testing and classification; he too would be traveling the same grim road as Jeff himself. And as a newcomer, he too would be under suspicion and scrutiny.

Jeff stopped short on a landing. He was suddenly aware that he had lost count of the flights he had gone down. He looked back to check his bearings, then moved around to the stairs moving up. The escalator creaked and groaned, as if every turn would be its last, and Jeff stared dreamily at the moving wall, waiting—until he passed the open well to the opposite stairs.

He froze, his mind was screaming. Unable to move, he stared at the pale, frightened face of the man on the down-going stairway. In the brief seconds while they passed, he stood rooted, completely paralyzed, unable to cry out. Then with a hoarse yell he turned. Half stumbling, half-falling, he ran down the up-going stairs until he finally reached the opening.

Then he vaulted across the barrier, crashing his shoulder against the wall as he went through. He caught a glimpse of the tall, slender figure running from the bottom of the stairs into the corridor at the bottom, and he shouted again in a burst of blinding rage. He took the steps three at a time, his mind numb to the pain as his foot struck the solid floor and twisted, sending him sprawling on his face. In an instant he was on his feet again, running, frantically, blindly, to the end of the corridor.

It broke into two hallways, going off in a Y. Both were dark and both were empty. Jeff stood panting, almost screaming out in rage, his whole body trembling. He started blindly down one corridor, jerked open a door and stared in at the small, empty office. He tried another door and another. Then he turned and ran back to the Y, spun around the corner and ran pell-mell down the second corridor. Only his own desperate footfalls echoed back to him in the darkness.

Back at the Y, he sank to the floor. Still panting, he

sobbed aloud in his rage, clenching his fists as he tried to regain control of his spinning mind. Rage there was—yes, and hatred and frustration. But also, tumbling through his mind in a wild, elated cadence, was a cry of sheer, incoherent savage joy. Because he knew now, beyond any shadow of doubt, that Paul Conroe was among the Mercy Men.

He looked up suddenly at the two figures approaching him from the lighted corridor. One of them held a tiny, deadly scorcher pistol trained on his chest. The other, a huge, burly man, reached down and jerked Jeff's face up into the light. "What's your unit?" the harsh voice grated.

Jeff glimpsed the gray cloth of the man's jacket, the official-looking black belt over his shoulder. "C unit," he panted.

The blow caught him full on the chin, twisting his head around with a jolt. "Wise guy, wandering around without a pass," the voice growled. "You scabs think you run the place, don't you?" Another blow struck him behind the ear, and a fist caught him hard in the pit of the stomach. As he doubled over retching, a smashing blow caught his chin, and he tasted blood in his mouth as his knees buckled under him.

He felt them, vaguely, half-carrying, half-dragging him down the corridor. He heard a door open and fell face down on the floor. A harsh voice said, "Here's your roommate, scut. Keep him home from now on." And the door slammed behind him.

Painfully, he raised himself on his hands, shook his head dazedly.

"You look like you're sick or something." The voice from the bed was hard and insolent.

Painfully, Jeff jerked his head up and stared. The girl blinked coldly and pulled a frazzled cigarette from her blue cotton shirt. She flicked a match with her thumb and touched off the smoke. Then she stared down at Jeff mockingly. "Sorry, Jack," said the girl called Blackie. "But it looks like we're roomies. So you might as well get used to the idea."

CHAPTER FOUR

SOMETHING exploded in Jeff's brain then, something he could no more control than the creeping, vicious hatred of Paul Conroe that had driven him for so long. The jangling, tinny music of the tavern was screaming through his mind; the indelible picture of the swerving, gyrating figure: the long raven hair, the impassive face, the full lips. His knees buckled and his head was reeling, but he lurched across the room at the girl. Catching her by the collar, he drew her face up to his with a wrench that knocked the cigarette from her hand and brought her breath out in a gasp.

"All right," he grated. "Where is he? Come on, come on...talk! Where is he? And don't tell me he's not here, because I know he is, understand? I just saw him. I just chased him, down below. He's here! I want to know where."

Her foot came up sharply and caught him in the leg, sending an agony of pain into his thigh. Suddenly she began to fight like a cat, clawing, biting—blue fire in her eyes. Jeff brought his hand up and slapped her face twice, hard. With a snarl she caught him in the stomach with her foot and tore herself free, sending him reeling back against the wall.

He bounded off, then stopped dead in his tracks. A horrible realization exploded in his mind. She was standing poised, her face twisted, her eyes burning, a stream of poisonous language pouring at him. In her hand was a knife, blade up, balanced in her hand with deadly intent. But Jeff hardly noticed the knife; he didn't hear the words as he stared unbelievingly at her face, his heart sinking. Because the face was wrong, somehow.

The lips were not right, the nose was shaped differently, the glow in the eyes was not right. His panting turned into a bitter sob of disbelief, of incredible disappointment. There couldn't be any doubt—it simply was not the right girl.

"Where—where is he?" he asked weakly, his heart pounding helplessly in his throat.

"Not another step," the girl snarled. "Another inch and I'll slice you up like putty."

"No, no—" Jeff shook his head, trying desperately to clear his mind, to understand. This was the girl he had seen in the visiphone screen. Yes, the same clothes, the same face. But she wasn't the girl in the tavern. "Conroe," he blurted out, plaintively. "You—you must know Conroe—"

"I've never heard of Conroe."

"But you must have—last night, in that dive—dancing—" Her jaw dropped as she stared at him in disgust. Then she gave the knife a flip into the desktop and sank down on her bed, her face relaxing. "Go away," she said tiredly. "That goddam Frenchman's sense of humor. Go on, beat it. I'm not rooming with any hoppy—at least until he's off the stuff.

"You don't know Conroe?"

The girl looked at him closely. "Look, Jack," she said with patient bitterness, "I don't know who you are and I don't know your pal Comstock or whatever it is. And I sure as hell wasn't dancing anywhere last night. I was working in the tank last night getting some looped-up hophead cooled off for the axe this morning. And it wasn't fun for either of us, and you'll be down there yourself if you don't cool off. And you won't like it, either. So go away, don't bother me."

Jeff sank down on the opposite bed, his head in his hands. "You—you looked so much like her—"

"So I looked so much like her!" She spat out a filthy word and drew her legs up, glaring at him.

Jeff reddened, his whole body aching. "All right, I'm

sorry. I got excited. I couldn't help it. And I can't leave here. I tried it a little while ago and ran into a couple of fists.

Blackie's lip curled. "The guards don't like us down here. They don't like anything about us. They'll kill you if you give them half an excuse."

Jeff looked up at her. "But why? I didn't do anything."

The girl laughed harshly. "Do you think that makes any difference to them? Look, Jack, let's face it: you're in a prison, understand? They don't call it that, and there aren't any bars. But you're not going anywhere, and the boys in gray are here to see that you don't. And they hate us because we're not good enough for them, and we're in line for the kind of money they don't dare go after. You're here for one thing: to make money, big money, or to get your brains jolted loose, and nothing else—" She looked up at him, her eyes narrowing. "Or are you?"

Jeff shook his head miserably. "No, nothing else. I'm waiting for testing. This other thing is an old fight, that's all. You wouldn't understand. You just looked so much like the girl—" He looked up at her, studying her face more closely. She wasn't as young as he had thought at first. There were little wrinkles around her eyes, a shade too much make-up showing where her mouth crinkled when she talked. Her lips were painted too full, and there was a tiredness in her eyes, a beaten, hunted look that she couldn't quite hide.

She leaned back on the bed, and even relaxation didn't erase the hardness. Only the jet-black hair and the smooth black eyebrows looked young and fresh.

Jeff shook his head and kept staring at her. "I don't get it," he said helplessly. "I was assigned to this room—"

"So was I." The girl's eyes hardened.

"Are you one of the…workers?"

She sneered bitterly. "You mean one of the experimental animals? That's right. The Mercy Men. Full of mercy, that's me." She spat on the floor.

"But the mixed company—"

There was no humor in her laugh. "What did you think, they'd have a separate boudoir for the ladies? How do they treat any kind of experimental animal? Get off it, Jack. They don't care what we do or how we live. All they want is good healthy human livestock when they're ready for it. Nothing more. That means they have to feed us and bunk us down. Period. And if you've got any wise ideas"—her eyes widened with a look of open viciousness, shocking in its intensity—"just try something. Just once. You'll find out a lot about Blackie in a hell of a rush." She rolled over contemptuously, turning her back to him. "You'll find out I don't like loonies for roommates, for instance."

Jeff lit a cigarette, his hands trembling. The room seemed to be spinning, and he felt his muscles sagging in pain and fatigue. He had counted so much on information from the girl. But incredible as the resemblance was, Blackie couldn't have been the girl he had seen in the tavern. If she had recognized him, he would have spotted it. She couldn't have hidden it completely.

Suddenly he felt terribly alone, almost beaten, helpless to go on. Where could he go? What could he do? How could he follow a trail that led straight into stone walls? He leaned back on the bed and yielded to the fatigue that plagued him. His mind sank into a confusion of hopelessness. Maybe, he thought wearily, maybe that plaguing doubt that lay in the fringes of his mind was right. Maybe he'd never find Conroe. He sighed as the darkness of utter exhaustion closed in on him, and his head sank back to the pillow—

He knew he was dreaming. Some tiny corner of his mind stood aside, prodding him, telling him he dare not sleep, that he must be up, moving, hunting, that the danger was too grave for sleep. But he slept, and the little corner of his mind prodded and cried out and watched...

He was walking along a brook, a walk he had taken once before, so very many years ago. A cool breeze struck down from the meadow, rumpling his hair. He heard the tinkle of the water as it sparkled across the rock. And he was afraid, so desperately afraid. The voice in his mind screamed out to him at every footstep, until he faltered and slowed and stopped.

Not here, Jeff, not here. Stop, stop now! If you go farther, you'll be dead—

Sweat broke out on his forehead. He tried to move forward, felt an iron grip on his legs. *Stop, Jeff, stop, you'll die, Jeff—* An overpowering wave of fear swept over him, and he turned. He ran like the wind, with the voice following him, crying out in his ear, following him on ghostly wings. In the dream he became a little boy again, running, screaming in fear. A man stood in his pathway, arms outstretched, and Jeff threw himself into his father's arms, sobbing as though his heart would break, clutching at him with incredible relief, burying his face in the strong, comforting chest. *Oh, daddy, daddy, you're safe. You're here, daddy.*

He looked up at his father's smiling face and he saw the strong, sensitive lines around the big man's mouth, the power and wisdom in the eyes. Nowhere else was there this sense of strength, of unlimited power, of complete comfort. He buried his face again in old Jacob Meyer's chest. A flood of deep peacefulness passed through his mind—

Jeff, Jeff, watch out!

He stiffened, his whole body going cold. The strong arms were no longer around him, and he was suddenly afraid again—afraid with a terror that bit deep into his mind. He looked up and screamed, a scream that echoed and reechoed. It came again and again—a scream of pure terror. Because his father's face was no longer next to him. There was another face, hanging bodiless and luminous above him. It was chalk white—a face of pure ghoulish evil, staring at him.

It was Conroe's face. He screamed again, tried to cover his eyes, tried to shrink down into nothing. But the hideous, twisted face followed him. The horrible fear intensified, sweeping through him like a flame, twisting into fiery hate in his heart, as he watched the evil, glowing face.

He killed your father, Jeff. He butchered your father, shot him down like an animal, in cold blood—

Jeff screamed and the evil face grinned and moved closer, until the rank breath was hot on Jeff's neck.

You must kill him, Jeff. He killed your father—

But why? Why did he do it, why…why…*why?* There was no answer. The voice trailed off into horrible laughter. Quite suddenly the face was gone. In its place was a tiny, distant figure—running, running like the wind, down the narrow, darkened hospital corridor. And Jeff was running too, burning with hatred, fighting desperately to catch up with the fleeing figure, to close the gap between them.

The walls were of gray stone. Conroe was running swiftly, unhindered. But horrid objects swept out of the walls at Jeff. He tripped on a wet, slimy thing on the floor and fell on his face. He scrambled up again as the figure disappeared around a far corner. The walls were gray and wet around him. He reached the Y, waiting, panting, screaming out his hatred down the empty, re-echoing hallways.

Then suddenly he glimpsed the figure and started running again, but they were no longer in the Hoffman Center. They were running down a hillside, a horrible, barren hillside, studded with long knives and spears and swords—shiny blades standing straight up from the ground, gleaming in the bluish light.

Conroe was far ahead, moving nimbly through the gauntlet of swords. But Jeff couldn't follow his path, for new knives sprang up before him, cutting his ankles, ripping his clothes. He panted, near exhaustion, as the figure vanished in the distance. Sinking down to the ground, Jeff sobbed, his whole body shaking. And the voice screamed mockingly in his ear: *You'll never get him, Jeff. No matter how hard you try, you'll never get him...never...never...never...*

But I've got to, I've got to. I've got to find him and kill him. Daddy told me to—

He woke with a jolt, his screams still echoing in the still room, sweat pouring from his forehead and body, soaking his clothes. He sat bolt upright. He searched for his watch, but couldn't find it. *How long had he slept?*

His eyes shot to the opposite bed, standing empty, and he rolled out onto his feet. He had the horrible feeling that the world had passed him by, that he had missed something critical while he slept.

He stared at his wrist. The watch was definitely gone. Then, with a curse, he crossed the room and ripped open Blackie's footlocker. Sure enough, the watch lay with the heap of gold jewelry on the dirty clothes pile. He stared at it as he re-strapped it on his wrist. Then he walked into the lavatory, splashed cold water into his face and tried to quell the fierce painful throbbing in his head. The watch said eight-thirty. He had slept for five hours—five precious hours for Conroe to hide, cover his tracks, disappear deeper into this mire of human trash.

Jeff stumbled to the door, glanced out to see two gray-clothed guards passing in the corridor. Quietly he pulled the door shut. His stomach was screaming from hunger and he searched the room restlessly. Finally, he unearthed a box of crackers and a quarter pound of cheese in the bottom of Blackie's locker. He ate ravenously and drank some water from the lavatory tap. Then he sank down on the edge of the bed.

The dream again, the same horrible, frightening, desperate dream—the dream that recurred and recurred; always different, yet always the same. The same face that had haunted him all his life, the face that had almost driven him insane that day, five years before, when he met it face to face for the first time; the face of the man he had hunted to the ends of the earth. But never had he caught the man, never had he seen him but for brief glimpses. Conroe had slipped from every trap before it was sprung. Yet finally he had become so desperate that he was forced to retreat down a one-way road that led to hellish death.

Jeff shook his head hopelessly as he tried to piece together the situation. He was in a half-world of avaricious men and women out to sell themselves for incredible fees. It was a half-world that seemed to Jeff only slightly more insane than the warped, intense world of pressure and fear and insecurity that lay outside the Hoffman Center. And in this half-world were a doctor who knew Jeff was a fraud, a kleptomaniac girl who thought he was an addict, and somewhere—the slender figure of the man he hunted.

Again he walked to the door. After peering out cautiously, he started down the corridor. From the far end he heard a burst of laughter, the sound of many voices. The smell of coffee floated down the corridor to tantalize him. He followed the sounds and reached the large, long room that served as a lounge and library for the Mercy Men in his unit.

The room was crowded. A dozen groups were huddled on the floor in a buzz of frantic excitement. The room was blue with cigarette smoke, and the lights glowed harshly from the walls. He saw the dice rolling in the centers of the groups and he also saw half a dozen tables, crowded with bright-eyed people. He heard the riffle of playing cards and the harsh, tense laugh of a winner drawing in a pot. And then he spied the Nasty Frenchman, his eyes bright with excitement, a cup of exceedingly black coffee in one hand and a pile of white paper tags in the other.

He grinned at Jeff with undisguised malice and said, "Come on in, wise guy. Things are just beginning to get hot."

Blinking, Jeff walked into the room.

CHAPTER FIVE

HIS FIRST impulse was to turn and run. There was no explaining it, no rationalizing the feeling of dread and danger that struck him as he walked into the room. The feeling swept over him with almost overpowering intensity; something was unbearably wrong here.

Jeff walked in slowly, closing the door behind him. The door seemed to be pulled tight shut, sucked out of his hand. That was when the tension in the air struck Jeff like an almost physical force, and his mind filled with dread.

No one noticed him. He stared around himself curiously. He watched the Nasty Frenchman shoulder his way through the crowd. One of Silly Giggin's particularly maddening nervous-jazz arrangements was squawking from a player somewhere in the room, and the air itself was filled with a jagged rattle of conversation that rose above the music.

Most of the faces were new to Jeff. There were tired, old ones, marked indelibly with lines of fear, lines of hunted hopelessness. There were faces with tight, compressed, bloodless lips; faces with eyes full of coldness and cynicism, and faces radiating sharp, perverted intelligence.

Crowds leaned tensely around the tables and watched the cards with eager, calculating eyes. Side bets were made as the hands were opened. Other groups huddled on the floor and watched the dice with beady, avaricious eyes.

The music jangled and scraped, and little bursts of harsh

laughter broke out to compete with it. And through it all ran the chilling inescapable feeling of error, of something missed, something gone horribly wrong.

He moved slowly through the room and searched the faces milling around him. His eyes caught Blackie's, far across the room, for the barest instant, and the chill of something gone wrong intensified and sent a quiver up his spine. He stopped a passerby and motioned at the nearest dice huddle. "How do you get in?" he asked.

The man shrugged, looking at him strangely. "You lay down your money and you play," he snapped. "If you got no money, then you've got the next job's payoff to bet with. 'Smatter, Jack, you new around here?" And the man moved on, shaking his head.

Jeff nodded, realization striking. What would be more natural to a group of people teetering from day to day on the brink of death? The need for excitement, for activity, would be overpowering in a dismal prison-place like this. And with the huge sums of money yet unearned to bet with— Jeff shuddered. Cut-throat games, yes, but could they really explain this strange tension he sensed? Or had something happened to change the atmosphere, to pervade every nook and cranny of the room with an air of explosive tension?

Jeff started moving toward the Nasty Frenchman. The little man was gulping coffee in the corner. He sucked on a long, black cigar and appeared to be in deep conversation with a bald-headed giant who leaned against the wall. Jeff spotted Blackie again. She was across the room on her knees. She faced a little buck-toothed man, as she swiftly rolled the three colored dice. Her eyes followed them, quick and un-naturally bright.

Jeff shook his head. Panmumjon was a high-speed, high-tension game—a game for the steel-nerved. Its famous dead-locks had often led to murder, as the pots rose higher and higher. The girl seemed to be winning. She rolled the dice with trance-like regularity, and the little buck-toothed man's face darkened as his money pile dwindled.

Across the room a corner crap game was moving swiftly, with staggering sums of money passing from hand to hand; the card games, though slower, left the mark of their tension on the players' faces. Jeff still stared, until he had seen every face in the room. Paul Conroe's face was not one of them.

No, he had not expected that. But what had happened? It was maddening to stand there, to feel the tension in the room, sense that it was growing until it seemed to pound at his temples. No one else seemed to notice it. Was he the only one aware of the change in the air, in the sounds, even in the color of the light against the walls? Something was impelling him, urging him to run, to get away, to leave the room now while he could. Yet when he tried to analyze the creeping, poisonous fear, tried to pin it down, it wriggled away into the fringes of his mind, and mocked him.

Finally, he reached the corner of the room. His ear caught the Nasty Frenchman's nasal voice, and he froze as he stared at the little man.

"I tell you, Harpo, I heard it with my own ears. You never saw Schiml so excited. And then Shaggy Parsons was saying that the whole unit was being split up—that's the A unit. I saw him when I was going through this afternoon. He was all excited, too."

"But why split it up?" The huge bald-headed man called Harpo growled, his heavy lips twisting in disgust. "I don't trust Shaggy Parsons for nothin', and I think you hear what you want to hear. What's the point to it? Schiml's coming along fine in the work he's using us in—"

The Nasty Frenchman turned red. "That's just it: we've been in and we're going to be out, right out in the cold. Can't you get that straight? Something's going to break. They're onto something—Schiml and his boys—something big. And they've got a new man, somebody they're excited about, somebody that's been knocking walls down just by looking at them, or something—"

Harpo made a disgusted noise. "You mean, the old ESP story again. So maybe they go off on another spook hunt. They'll get over it, same as they did the last time or the time before."

The Nasty Frenchman's voice was tense. "But they're *changing things*. And changes mean trouble." He glanced at Jeff and his eyebrows went up. "Look, they get on a line of work, they assign men to different parts of a job, they get work lined up months in advance. Then all of a sudden something new comes along. They get excited about something and they toss out a couple dozen workers, add a couple dozen new ones, change fees, change the work. And they end up giving the best pay to somebody who's just come in. I don't like it. I've been here too long. I've had too many tough, lousy jobs here to just get pushed aside because they don't happen to be interested anymore in what they were doing to me before. And they never tell us. We never know for sure. We just have to wait and guess and hope."

The little man's eyes blazed. "But we can pick up some things, a little here, a little there—you learn how, after a while. And I can tell you, something's wrong, something's going to happen. You can even feel it in here."

Jeff's skin crawled. That was it, of course. There was something wrong. But it hadn't happened yet. It was going to happen. He stared at a huddled group around a pan-mumjon game, watched the bright-colored dice cubes roll across and back, across and back. A newcomer, the Nasty Frenchman had said, someone who had come in and disrupted the smooth work schedule of the Center, someone who had the doctors suddenly excited. Someone whom they were planning to use—on a spook hunt.

What kind of a spook hunt? Why that choice of words? Could Conroe conceivably be the newcomer they had been talking about? It didn't seem possible that it could have happened so suddenly if Conroe were the one—but who? And what did this have to do with the ever-growing sense of impending danger that pervaded the room, right now?

Jeff's eyes wandered to the dice game, and the fear in his mind suddenly grew to a screaming torrent. *Go away, Jeff. Don't watch, don't look*— He scowled, suddenly angry. Why not look? What was there so dangerous in a dice game? He moved over to the nearby huddle and watched the moving cubes in fascination. *No, Jeff, no, don't do it, Jeff*— With a curse, he dropped to his knees and reached out for the dice.

"You in?" somebody asked. Jeff nodded, his face like a rock. The voice had stopped screaming in his ear, and now something else grew in his mind: a wild exhilaration that caught his breath and swept through his brain like a whirl-wind. His eyes sparkled and he pulled money from his pocket. He laid the bills on the floor and his hands closed on the dice.

He faced a little, pimple-faced man with beady black eyes and he raised the three brightly colored dice, rolling into the familiar pattern. The dice deadlocked in four throws. He sweated out seven more with new dice. Then Jeff saw a break in the odds, boosted the ante on his next throw and caught his breath as the man facing him matched it.

The dice rolled, fell into deadlock again, and the crowd around them gasped, moved in closer around them. The third set of dice was brought out, for the attempts at deadlock-breaking. Then a fourth set followed, as the complex structure of the game built up like a house of cards. Then Jeff's dice at last rolled the critical number, and the structure began to break apart—throw after throw falling faster and faster into his hands.

Four or five people moved in at his side with side bets and began to collect along with him, as he moved into another game, built it up. This one he lost cold, but still he played on, his excitement growing.

And then, suddenly, pandemonium broke loose in the room. Eyes glanced up, startled, at the two men, far across the room, who stood facing each other, eyes blazing.

"Throw them down! Go on! Throw them, see how they land!"

Somebody shouted, "What happened, Archie?"

"He's got loaded dice in here, somehow." Archie pointed an accusing finger at the other man. "They don't fall right. There's something wrong with them—"

The other man snarled. "So you aren't winning any more—so what? You brought the dice in yourself."

"But the odds aren't right. Something funny is going on."

Jeff turned back to the dice, his mind still screaming, sensing that disaster hung in the air like a heavy sword. His own game moved on, faster and faster. Somewhere across the room another fight broke out, and another. Several men dropped out of games and stood up against the walls. Their eyes were wide with anger as they watched the other players. And then Jeff rolled three sixes, fourteen times in a row. He tossed the dice down in front of his gaping opponents with a curse and walked shakily back to the corner. The whole room spun around his head.

Suddenly, in this room, probabilities had gone mad. He could feel the shifting instability of the atmosphere, as real and oppressive to him as if it were solid and he were attempting to wade through it. This was what had been bothering him, plaguing him. Quite suddenly and without explanation, something impossible had begun to happen. Cards had begun to fall in unbelievable sequences, repeating themselves with idiotic regularity; dice had defied the laws of gravity as they spun on the tables and floor.

A hubbub filled the room as the players stopped and stared at each other, unable to understand the impossible that was happening before them. Then Blackie was passing Jeff, her face flushed, a curious light of desperation in her eyes.

An impulse passed through Jeff's mind. He reached out an arm, stopped the girl. "Game," he said sharply.

Her eyes flashed at him. "What game?"

"Anything." He held up his wrist before her eyes and showed her the gold watch. "We can play for this."

Something flared in her eyes for a moment before she gained control. Then she was down on her knees, pushing her sleeves up, a tight look of fear and dread haunting her eyes as she looked up at Jeff. "Something's happening," she said softly. "The dice—they're not right."

"I know it. Why not?" His voice was hoarse, his eyes hard on her face.

She threw him a baffled look. "There isn't any reason. Nothing is different, but the dice don't fall right. That's all, they just don't."

Jeff grinned tightly. "Go on, throw them."

She threw the dice, saw them dance on the floor, caught her number. Jeff rolled them, beat her on it, picked up the money. He rolled again, then again. The tightness grew around the girl's eyes; little tense lines hardened near her mouth. Nervously, she fumbled a cigarette into her mouth, lit it, puffed as the dice rolled.

She lost. She lost again. Side bets picked up around them, the people as they watched catching the tension that was building up.

"What's happening?"

"The dice—my God! They've gone crazy!"

"Blackie's losing. What do you think—"

"—losing? She never loses on dice. Who's the guy?"

"Never saw him before. Look, he took another one! Those dice are hexed."

"My cards were crazy too: king high full every time, a dozen hands in a row. How can you bet on something like that, I ask you."

The Silly Giggins record screeched louder, then gave a squawk as the record suddenly shattered in a thousand pieces. Somebody cursed and threw a pack of cards on the floor, and a scream broke out across the room. One group came suddenly to blows; several dice games tightened down to bloody conflict between individuals. A man burst into tears, suddenly, and sat back on his haunches, his face stricken. "They can't act this way," he wailed. "They just *can't*—"

Jeff's eyes watched the spinning dice, and again something was screaming in his ear. He felt as though his head was going to burst, but he continued to roll and he saw the girl's face darken with each throw. He saw the fear shine out from her blue eyes. Suddenly she let out a curse, snatched the dice from Jeff's hand and threw them sharply across the room. She stared at Jeff venomously, then glared at the people around her as if she were a cornered animal.

"It's all of you," she snarled. "You're turning them against me. You're making them fall wrong." She spat on the floor and started for the door. Jeff moved after her but felt a restraining hand on his arm.

"Leave her alone," said the Nasty Frenchman. "You'll have trouble on your hands if you don't. You see what I meant about something being wrong? The whole crowd here is on edge, as if somebody were picking them up and throwing them down. Who ever saw dice fall that way, or cards fall that way"—the little man's eyes flashed slyly—*"unless somebody was controlling them."*

Jeff's breath was faster as he stared at the Nasty Frenchman, and his voice was hoarse. "What are you talking about?"

The little man's lips twisted angrily. "You saw what happened in here, didn't you?"

Jeff turned away in anger. He wove through the crowd, his jaw tight as he moved toward the door. The Nasty Frenchman could only glimpse the truth, but someone else saw more, much more. Somehow, Jeff knew that this past hour held the key to the whole problem, if he could only see it. Here was the answer to the whole tangled puzzle of the girl and Paul Conroe, of Dr. Schiml and the Mercy Men.

And he knew that when he reached the room, the girl would be waiting. She would be waiting with cold fire in her eyes, as she sat at the table, a small pair of colored dice lying before her in the dim light.

Jeff hurried down the darkened corridor, fear exploding in his brain. She would be there and he knew why she would be smoldering when he walked into the room. He had seen her eyes and face as they had thrown the dice. He knew beyond any shadow of doubt who had been controlling the dice.

The girl was waiting, just as he had known she would. He stepped into the room and closed the door gently behind him, facing her desperate eyes as she rolled the colored dice back and forth in front of her. "Game," she challenged, her voice harsh and metallic.

The room was tense with silent fear as he sank down opposite her, at the table.

CHAPTER SIX

JEFF REACHED out and took the dice from the girl's hand. "Put them away, Blackie," he said softly. "You don't have to prove anything. I know—"

"Game," she repeated harshly, shaking her head.

"Look. Think a minute. Back there, do you know what happened in that room?"

Her eyes caught his and were wide with fear. "Game," she whispered, her hands trembling. "You've got to play me!"

He shrugged, his eyes tired as he watched her face. He took the dice and rolled them out on the table. A three, a four and a five fell; he saw her eyes flash across the table, taking in the sequence. Then her hand reached out, grasped the dice, and gave them a throw. The hostility in her mind struck out at him, reinforcing the terrible dread that he already felt. He fought the hostility, staring at the dice, his hands gripping the edge of the table. And the dice danced and settled down: a three, a four and a five...

The girl's eyes widened, staring first at him, then back at the dice. Slowly she reached out, took the cube with the five showing, sent it bouncing across the table. It spun and bounced—and settled down once again with the five exposed.

Jeff felt the blast of bitter fear strike out from the girl's eyes. The room seemed to scream with the tension he felt. She took the dice with trembling hands, threw them out hard and clenched her fists as they fell. The three and four settled out immediately. Jeff watched the third cube, spinning on one corner, spinning... spinning... He felt his muscles grow tense, his mind screaming, tightening down as he stared at the little cube. It was as though an iron fist held his brain in its palm and was slowly, slowly squeezing. And the little cube continued, ridiculously, to spin and spin, until it suddenly flipped over onto its side and lay still with the five exposed.

Blackie gave a choked scream, her face pasty white.

"Then it was you." She choked, staring at him as if he were a ghost. "You were doing it deliberately in there, throwing off the odds, twisting things around, turning the dice against me."

Jeff shook his head violently. "No, no, not me—us—both of us. We were fighting each other, without knowing it—"

Her hand went up to her mouth, choking off the words as she stared at him. Jeff stared at the dice, his whole body trembling, huge drops of sweat running down his forehead. And as he watched, the dice hopped about on the table, like jumping beans, turning over and over, jerkily, spinning on their edges in a horrible, incredible little dance. Jeff shook his head, his eyes wide with horror as he watched the dice.

"You knew it all along," the girl choked. "You came in there just to torment me, to show me up—"

"No, no." Jeff turned wide eyes on her. "I didn't know it, until I picked up the dice in that room. Something drove me to do it. I didn't know what I was doing until all of a sudden the dice were doing what I wanted them to do—" He broke off, panting. "I never knew it, I never dreamed it." His eyes sought the girl's, pleading. "I didn't understand it; I couldn't help it. I just knew that something wrong was going on. And then I knew that somebody was fighting me. There was a tension in it. I felt it. I knew somebody was tampering with the dice. Then when I got near you, I knew it was you."

The girl's face was working, tears welling up in her eyes. "I had to—I had to win with them."

"Then you knew you were doing it!" Jeff stared at her. "And when both of us started tampering, opposing each other, the probabilities governing the games went wild, completely, wild."

The girl was sobbing, her face in her hands. "I could always control it. It always worked. It was the only thing I could do that came out right. Everything else has always gone wrong." She sobbed like a baby, her shoulders shaking as she choked out great, racking sobs.

Jeff leaned forward, almost cruelly, his eyes burning at her.

"When did you find out you could…make dice fall the way you wanted them to?"

The girl shook her head helplessly. "I didn't know it. I didn't have any idea, until I came here. It was the only thing I could win at. Everything else I lost at. All my life I've been losing."

"What have you been losing?"

"Everything, everything—everything I touch turns black, goes sour, somehow."

"But what, *what?*" Jeff leaned toward the girl, his voice hoarse. "Why did you come here? How did you get here?"

The girl's sobs broke out again, her shoulders shaking in anguish. "I don't know, I don't know. Oh, I could take it, up to a limit, but then I couldn't stand it any more. Everything I tried went wrong; everyone that was near me went wrong too. Even the rackets wouldn't work with me around."

"What rackets?"

Her voice was weak and cracking. "Any of the rackets. I've been in a dozen, two dozen, ever since the war. Dad was killed in the first bombing of the Fourth War, when I was just a kid—twelve, thirteen, I can't remember now. He died trying to get us out of the city and through to the Defense area north of the Trenton section. Radiation burns got him, maybe pneumonia, I don't know. But it got Dad first and Mom later."

She straightened up and wiped her eyes with her sleeve. "We never did get out of the devastated area. We were killing dogs and cats for food for a while. Then when things did get straightened out, we ran into the inflation, the burned-out crops, the whole rat race. The dirty breaks were coming in hard then. First we were guerrillas, then we were bushwhackers. Then we came into the city again and started shaking down the rich ones that came back from the mountains where they hid."

"But you came in here," Jeff grated. "Why here, if you were doing so well in rackets?"

"I wasn't. Can't you understand? The luck—it was running wrong, worse and worse all the time. And then I got hooked on dope. Narcotics control was all shot to pieces during the war; heroin was all over the place. But they knew I had this hard-luck jinx. They caught me on it, until I was hooked bad."

She shrugged, her face a study in pathetic hopelessness. "They hauled me in here. Schiml sold me his bill of goods. What could I lose? I was so tired, I didn't care. I didn't care if they jolted my brains loose, or what they did to me. All I wanted was to eat and get off the dope and get enough cash so I could try for something decent, where hard luck couldn't touch me. And I didn't really care if I never got out."

"But with the dice you made out."

"Oh, yes, with the dice—" The girl's eyes flickered for a moment. "I found out I could make them sit up and talk for me. I played it cozy, didn't let anybody catch on. But they always worked for me, until tonight—"

Jeff nodded, his face white. "Until tonight, when you found out you were fighting for control. Because tonight I found out they'd talk for me too. And you couldn't beat me with them."

Her voice was weak. "I—I couldn't budge them. They fell the way you called them."

"It isn't possible, you know," Jeff said softly. "Every time they've tried to prove it was, they've found some loophole in the study of it, something wrong somewhere. Nobody's ever proved a thing about psychokinesis."

The girl grinned mirthlessly. "They've been trying to prove it here since the year one. Every now and again they get hot on it. They've just tested somebody that's got them excited and they'll be starting the whole works over again."

Jeff leaned over, his eyes blazing. "Yes, yes, who's that person?"

"I don't know. I just heard it.

A new recruit, I guess."

"A recruit named Conroe?"

Her eyes widened at the virulence in his voice. "I—I don't know, I don't know. I've only heard. I don't even know if there is such a person."

"Where can I find out?"

Again the fear was in her eyes. "I—I don't know."

Jeff's voice was tense, his eyes fixed on the girl's face in desperate eagerness. "Look, you've got to help me. I know he's here. I must find him. I saw him this afternoon. Remember when the guards brought me in here? I saw him on the stairs. I chased him and lost him, but he's here. He's hiding, running away from me. I've got to find him, somehow. Please, Blackie, you can help me."

Her eyes were wide on his face. "What do you want with him? Why are you after him? I don't want to get mixed up in anything—"

"No, no, it won't mix you up. Look, I want to kill him. Short and sweet, nothing more—just kill him. I want to send one bullet into his brain, watch his face splatter out, watch his skull break open. That's all I want, just one bullet—"

Jeff's voice was low, the words wrenched from his throat, and the hatred in his eyes was poisonous as it washed over the girl's face. "He haunts me, for years he's haunted me." Jeff's voice dropped, the words breaking the stillness of the room in a hoarse, terrible cadence. "He killed my father. This Conroe—he butchered my father like an animal, shot him down in cold blood. It was horrible, ruthless. Conroe was the assassin. He killed my father without a thought of mercy in his mind. And I loved my father, I loved him with all the love I had." He stared at the girl. "I'll kill the man that killed my father if I have to die myself in the killing."

"And that man is here?"

"That man is here. I've hunted him for years. This was his last resort, his final desperate gamble for escape. He had nowhere else to turn. I've got the outside tied up so that he doesn't dare to leave. Now I've got to track him down in here. I've got to find him and kill him, before I'm caught, before I'm tested and classified. I've got to move fast and I need help. I need help so much."

The girl leaned toward him, her eyes dark as she stared at him. "The dice," she said softly. "I've been playing it cozy. I still could—if you'll let me."

His eyes widened. "Anything you say," he said. "We'll play it cozy together. But I've got to have floor plans of the place, information on how to avoid the guards. I've got to know where their records are kept, their lists and rosters and working plans."

"Then it's a deal?"

His eyes caught hers, and for an instant he saw something behind the mask she wore, something of the fear that lay in there, something of a child who fought against impossible odds to find a toehold in the world. Then the barrier was back up, and her eyes were blank and revealed nothing.

Jeff held out his hand, touched her palm lightly and clenched her fingers. "It's a deal," he said.

The trip down the corridor was a nightmare. Jeff's mind was still reeling from the incredible discovery of the dice, the sudden, unbelievable awareness that he and Blackie had been silently and fiercely battling each other for control, fighting with a fury that had somehow shattered the very warp of probability in the room where they had been. How could he have had a part in something like this? He had never had reason to suspect he might carry such a power, yet here was evidence he could not disregard. And how could it fit into the question of Paul Conroe, and the mysterious recruit to the Mercy Men who had just been tested?

A thought struck Jeff, quite suddenly. It came with such impact that he stopped cold in his tracks. It was so simple, so impossible, yet no more impossible than the things he had already seen with his own eyes. Because the incredible record of escapes that Conroe carried, the impossible regularity with which Conroe had managed to avoid capture, time after time, seemed too much to accept as coincidence. And if Conroe were indeed carrying latent extra-sensory powers, he could continue to slip from trap after trap—*unless Jeff could oppose those powers with powers of his own.*

Jeff cursed in his teeth. How could he tell? He had no evidence that Conroe carried any extra-sensory power whatsoever, and surely there was little enough to indicate that he had any more than most latent powers. There were so many, many possibilities, and so little concrete evidence to go on.

And if Conroe had such powers, why had he been so startled to meet Jeff on the stairs? Why the look of fear and disbelief that had streaked across his face? Jeff glanced at his watch, saw the minute hand move to eleven-thirty. He would have to hurry, for the guards would be down the escalator in a few moments. And these thoughts of his could lead to nowhere. Conroe had been jolted to see Jeff. It must have been a horrible shock for him to realize that the Hunter had followed him, even into this death trap, to know that the Hunter would have the outside so well guarded that he, the Hunted, could never get out. Now Conroe would be forced to gamble against being caught and assigned to work as a Mercy Man. Yes, it must have been a horrible jolt for Conroe, driving one last, searing bolt of fear into his already desperate mind. And what would he have tried to do?

A thousand ideas flooded Jeff's mind. He was waiting for

testing. Perhaps Conroe, somehow, had been tested already? Could Jeff succeed in stalling Schiml, especially if the rumors spinning down the dark corridors were true? There was no sure way of telling. All Jeff could do was to search the file rooms Blackie had directed him to.

He stopped at the entrance to the escalator, pored over the floor plan Blackie had sketched for him. He spotted the escalator, oriented himself on the plan. The filing rooms were two flights below. If he could reach them without being stopped… He moved silently onto the down shaft, his eyes moving constantly for a sight of a gray-garbed prowler.

At the foot of the escalator he stopped short. Three men in white were pushing a gurney along the corridor. Jeff glanced at the twitching form under the blankets. Then he looked away hurriedly. One of the men dropped behind and waved at him sharply as he stepped off the stairs. The man still wore the operating mask hanging from his neck, and his hair was tightly enclosed in the green-knit operating cap.

The doctor tipped a thumb over his shoulder and pointed down the corridor. "You coming to fix the pump?"

Jeff blinked rapidly. "That's right," he croaked. "Did— did Terry come with the tools yet?"

"Nobody came in yet. We just finished. Been in there since three this afternoon, and the damned pump went ker-flooey right in the middle. Had to aspirate the poor joe by hand, and if you think *that's* not a job—" The doctor wiped sweat from his forehead. "Better get it fixed tonight. We've got another one going in at eight in the morning and we've got to have the pump."

Jeff nodded, and started down the hall, his heart thudding madly against his ribs. He reached the open door to one of the operating rooms. Slipping into the small dressing-room annex, he snatched one of the gowns and caps from the wall.

If they were still operating this late, it was a heaven-sent chance. No guard would bother him if he were wearing the white of a doctor or the green of a surgeon. He struggled into the clumsy gowning, tying it quickly behind his back, and slipped the cap over his head. Finally he found a mask, snapped it up under his ears as he had seen it worn by the doctors in the corridors.

In a moment he was back on the escalator, descending to the next floor. At the foot of the stairs, he started quickly down the corridor Blackie had indicated, glancing at each door as he passed. The first two had lights under them, indicating that these apparently were operating rooms still in use. Finally he stopped before a large, heavy door, with a simple sign painted on the wooden panel: COMPUTER TECHNICIANS ONLY. He tried the door, found it locked. Quickly he glanced up and down the corridor, doubled a hard fist and drove it through the panel with a crunch. Then he fumbled inside for the lock.

In an instant he was inside. The torn hole in the panel glared at him. He threw the door wide open and snapped on the lights, throwing the room into bright fluorescent light. Then he drew the pale-green gown closer about him and moved across the room to the huge file panel that faced him.

It was not his first experience with the huge punched-card files that had become so necessary in organizations where the numbers and volumes of records made human operatives too slow or clumsy. Quickly Jeff moved to the mastercontrol panel, searched for the section and coding system for Research: Subject Personnel.

First he would try the simple coding for Conroe's name, on the chance that Conroe had come in using his own name. Jeff rechecked the coding, punched the buttons which would relay through the cards alphabetically; then he waited as the machinery whirred briefly. A panel lighted near the bottom of the control board, spelling the two words: NO

INFORMATION.

Jeff's fingers sped over the coding board again, as he started coding in a description. He coded in height, weight, eye color, hair color, bone contour, lip formation—every other descriptive category he could think of. Then again he punched the "Search" button.

This time several dozen cards fell down. He picked them up from the yield-slot and slowly leafed through them, glancing both at the small photograph attached to each card and at the small "date of admission" code symbol at the top of each card. Again he found nothing. Disgusted, he tried the same system again, this time adding two limiting coding symbols: Subject Personnel and Recent Admission. And again the cards were negative. Not a single one could possibly have been connected with Paul Conroe.

Jeff sat down at the desk facing the panel and he searched his mind for another pathway of identification. Suddenly a thought occurred to him. He searched through his pocket for a picture wallet, drew out the small, ID-size photo of Conroe that he carried for identification purposes.

Searching the panel, he finally found the slot he was looking for: the small, photo electronic chamber for recording picture identification. He slipped the photo into the slot, punched the "Search" button, and waited again, his whole body tense.

The machine buzzed for a long moment. Then a single card dropped into the slot. Eagerly Jeff snatched it up, stared down at the attached photograph, which almost perfectly matched the photo from his pocket. Near the top of the card was a small typewritten notation: Conroe, Paul A., INFORMATION RESTRICTED. ALL FILE NOTATIONS RECORDED IN HOFFMAN CENTER CENTRAL ARCHIVES.

Below this notation was a list of dates. Jeff read them,

staring in disbelief, then read them again. Incredible, those dates—dates of admission to the Hoffman Center and dates of release. It was impossible that Conroe could have been here at the times the dates indicated: ten years ago, when the Hoffman Center was hardly opened; five years ago, during the very time when Jeff had been tracking him down. Yet the dates were there, in black and white, cold, impersonal, indisputable. And below the dates was a final notation, inked in by hand: CENTRAL ARCHIVES CLASSIFICATION: ESP RESEARCH.

Swiftly Jeff stuffed the card into his shirt. He refiled the other cards with trembling fingers, his heart pounding a frightful tattoo in his forehead. Incredible, yet he knew, somehow, that it fit into the picture, that it was a key to the picture. He turned, started for the door, and stopped dead.

"Schiml!" he breathed.

The figure lounged against the door, green cap askew on his head, mask still dangling about his neck. There was a smile on his face as he leaned back, regarding Jeff in amusement. Nonchalantly, he tossed a pair of dice into the air, and caught them, still smiling. "Let's go, Jeff," said Dr. Schiml. "We've got some tests to run."

"You—you mean, in the morning," Jeff stammered, hardly believing his ears.

The smile broadened on the doctor's lips, and he gave the dice another toss and dropped them in his pocket. "Not in the morning, Jeff," he said softly. "Now."

CHAPTER SEVEN

JEFF SANK down in the chair, his forehead streaming sweat. He clenched his fists as he tried to regain control of his trembling muscles. *How long had Schiml been standing there? Just a second or two? Or had he been watching Jeff for ten* minutes, watching him punch down the filing codes, watching him stuff the filing card into his shirt? There was nothing to be told from the doctor's face, as the man smiled down at his trembling quarry. There was nothing in the eyes of the guards who stood behind him in the hallway, their hands poised on their heavy sidearms.

Schiml turned to one of them, nodded slightly, and they disappeared, their boots clanging in the still corridor behind them. Then he turned his eyes back to Jeff, the ghost of a knowing smile still flickering about his eyes. "Find anything interesting?" he asked, his eyes narrowing slightly.

Jeff fumbled a cigarette to his lips, gripped the lighter to steady it. "Nothing to speak of," he said hoarsely. "Been a long time since I worked one of these files." His eyes caught Schiml's defiantly, held them in desperation. Finally Schiml blinked and looked away.

"Looking for anything special?" he asked smoothly.

"Nothing special." Jeff blew smoke out into the room, his trembling nerves quieting slightly.

"I see. Just sight-seeing, I suppose."

Jeff shrugged. "More or less. I wanted to see the setup."

A dry smile crossed Schiml's face. "Particularly the setup in the filing room," he said softly. "I thought I'd find you here. Blackie said you'd just stepped out for a short walk, so we just took a guess." The doctor's eyes hardened sharply on Jeff's face. "And all dressed up like a doctor, too."

He stepped across the room, jerked the cap from Jeff's head, snapped the string to the gown with a sharp swipe of his hand. "We don't do this around here," he said, his voice cutting like a razor. "Doctors wear these, nobody else. Got that straight? We also do not wander around breaking into filing rooms, just looking at the setup. If the guards had caught you at it, you wouldn't be alive right now—which would have been a dirty shame, since we have plans for you."

He jerked his thumb toward the door. "After you, Jeff. We've got some work to do tonight."

Jeff moved out into the hall, took up beside the tall doctor as he started back for the escalator. "You weren't serious about testing me tonight, surely."

Dr. Schiml stared at him. "And why not?"

"Look, it's late. I'll be here in the morning."

The doctor walked on in silence for a long moment. Jeff followed, his mind racing, a thousand questions tumbling through in rapid succession: questions he dared not ask, questions he couldn't answer. How much did Schiml know? And how much did he suspect? A chill ran down Jeff's back. What had he been doing with the dice? Could Blackie possibly have told him? Or could he have heard about the freakish occurrence in the game room through other channels? And what could he learn in the course of the testing that he didn't know already?

Jeff puzzled as he matched the doctor's rapid pace. They went up the escalator, down the twisting corridor toward an area beyond the living quarters that Jeff hadn't seen before. Above all, he must keep his nerve, keep a tight control on his tongue, on his reactions, make sure that there were no tricks to tear information from him that he didn't dare divulge.

He looked at Schiml, sharply, a frown on his face. "I still don't see why this can't wait 'til morning. Why the big hurry?"

Schiml stopped, turned to Jeff in exasperation. "You still think we're running a picnic grounds here, don't you?" he snapped. "Well, we're not. We're doing a job, a job that can't wait for morning or anything else. We work a twenty-four-hour schedule here. All you do is provide the wherewithal to work with—nothing more."

"But I'll be tired, nervous. I don't see how I could pass any kind of test."

Schiml laughed shortly. "These aren't the kind of tests you pass or fail. Actually, the more tired and nervous you are, the better the results will be for you. They'll give you an extra edge of safety when you're assigned to a job. What the tests tell us is what we can expect from you, the very minimum. Basically, we're working to save your life for you."

Jeff blinked at him, followed him through swinging doors into a long, brightly lighted corridor, with green walls and a gleaming tile floor, "What do you mean, save my life? You seem to delight in just the opposite here, from what I've heard."

The doctor made an impatient noise. "You got the wrong information," he said angrily. "That's the trouble. You people insist upon listening to and believing the morbid stories, all the unpleasantness you hear about the work here. And it's all either completely false or only half-truth. This business of bloodthirstiness, for instance. It's just plain not true.

"One of the biggest factors in our work here is making arrangements for optimum conditions for the success of our experiments. By 'optimum' we mean the best conditions from several standpoints; from the standpoint of what we're trying to learn—the experiment itself, that is—and from the standpoint of the researcher, too. But most particularly, we're working for optimum recovery odds for the experimental animals--you, in this case."

Jeff snorted. "But still, we're just experimental animals, from your viewpoint," he said sharply.

"Not just experimental animals," Schiml snapped angrily. "You're the experimental animals. Working with human beings isn't the same as working with cats and dogs and monkeys—far from it. Dogs and cats are stronger and tougher, more durable than humans, which is why they're used for preliminary work of great success. But basically, they're expendable. If something goes wrong, that's too bad.

But we've learned something, and the dog or cat can be sacrificed without too many tears. But we don't feel quite the same about human beings."

"I'm glad to hear that," said Jeff sourly. "It makes me feel better."

"I'm not trying to be facetious. I mean it. We're not ghouls. We don't have any less regard for human life than anyone else, just because we're responsible for some human death in the work we're doing. For one thing, we study every human being we use, try to dig out his strengths and weaknesses, physical and mental. We want to know how he reacts to what, how fast he recuperates, how much physical punishment his body can take, how far his mental resiliency will extend. Then when we know these things, we can fit him into the program of research that will give him the very best chance of coming out in one piece. At the same time, he will fill a spot that we need filled. No, there's no delight here in taking human life or jeopardizing human safety."

They turned abruptly off the corridor and entered a small office. Schiml motioned Jeff to a chair, sat himself down behind a small desk and began sorting through several stacks of forms. The room was silent for a moment. Then the doctor punched a button on the telephone panel.

When the light blinked an answer to him, he said: "Gabe? He's here. Better come on up."

Then he flipped down the switch and leaned back, lighting a long, slender cigar and undoing the green robe around his neck.

Jeff watched him, still puzzling over what he had just said. The doctor seemed so matter-of-fact. What he had said made sense, but somewhere in the picture there seemed to be a gaping hole. "This sounds like it's a great setup—for you doctors and researchers," he said finally. "But what's it leading to? What good is it doing? Oh, I know, it increases your knowledge of men's minds, but how does it help the man in the street? How does it actually help anyone, in the long run? How do you ever get the government to back it with the financial mess they're facing in Washington?"

Schiml threw back his head and laughed aloud. "You've got the cart before the horse," he said, when he got control of his voice. "Support? Listen, my lad, the government is running itself bankrupt just to keep our research going. Did you realize that? *Bankrupting itself!* And why? Because unless our work pays off—and soon—there isn't going to be any government left. That's why. Because we're fighting something that's eating away at the very roots of our civilization, something that's creeping and growing and destroying."

He stared at Jeff, his eyes wide. "Oh, the government knows that the situation is grave. We had to prove it to them, show it to them time and again, until they couldn't miss it any longer. But they saw it finally. They've seen it growing for a century or more, ever since the end of the Second War. They've seen the business instability, the bank runs and the stock market dives. They've seen the mental and moral decay in the cities. They could see it, but it took statistics to prove that there was a pattern to it, a pattern of decay and rot and putrefaction that's been crumbling away the clay feet of this colossal civilization of ours."

The doctor stood up, paced back and forth across the room and sent blue smoke into the air from the cigar as he walked. "Oh, they support us all right. We don't know for sure what we're fighting, but we do know the answer is in the functioning of the minds and brains of man. We're working against a disease—a creeping disease of men's minds—and we are forced to use men to search those minds, to study them, to try to weed out the poison of the disease. And so we have the Mercy Men to help us fight."

The doctor's lips twisted in a bitter sneer as he sat heavily down on the chair again, crunched the cigar out viciously in the tray. "Mercy Men who have no mercy in their souls, who have no interest nor concern with what they're doing, or what it may be accomplishing. They are interested in one thing only: the amount of money they'll be paid for having their brains jogged loose."

The scorn was heavy in Dr. Schiml's eyes. "Well, we don't care who we have: addicts, condemned murderers, prostitutes, the trash from the skid-row gutters. They're all drawn here, like flies to a dunghill. But they're here on errands of mercy, whether they like it or not, or know it or not. And we take them because they're the only ones who can be bought, and we guard them for all we're worth, so that the goal will be accomplished." He took a deep breath and stared scornfully at Jeff. "That's you I'm talking about, you know."

Jeff's hands trembled as he snuffed out his smoke. He stood up as the corridor door opened, admitting a small, dark-haired man with thick glasses. He was dressed in doctor's whites. Jeff rubbed his chest nervously and took a deep breath, still acutely aware of the stiff card in his shirt front.

"All right," he said hoarsely, "so you're talking about me. When do we get started with this?"

The little dressing room was cramped; it reeked of anesthetic. Jeff walked in, followed by Dr. Schiml and the other doctor, and started removing his shoes. "This is Doctor Gabriel," Schiml said, indicating his myopic colleague. "He'll start you off with a complete physical. Then you'll have a neurological. Come on into the next room as soon as you're undressed." And with that the two doctors disappeared through swinging doors into an inner room.

Jeff removed his shirt and trousers swiftly, carefully folding the file card and stuffing it under the innersole of his right shoe. It wasn't exactly the perfect hiding place, if anyone were looking for the card. But not once during the conversation had Schiml's eyes strayed curiously to Jeff's shirtfront. Either Schiml had not seen him take the card, or else the doctor's self-control was superhuman. And no mention of the dice had been made, either. Jeff gave his shoes a final pat, tossed his clothes on one of the gurneys lining the walls and pushed through the doors into the next room.

It was huge, dome ceiling, with a dozen partitions dividing different sections from one another. One end looked like a classroom, with blackboards occupying a whole wall. Another section carried the paraphernalia of a complete gymnasium. The doctors were sitting in a corner that was obviously outfitted as an examination room: the tables were covered with crisp green sheeting, and the walls had gleaming cabinets full of green-wrapped bundles and instruments.

Schiml sat on the edge of a desk. His eyes watched Jeff closely as he lit a cigarette, leaned back and blew rings into the air. Dr. Gabriel motioned Jeff to the table and started the physical without further delay.

It was the most rigorous, painstaking physical examination Jeff had ever had. The little, squinting doctor poked and probed him from head to toe. He snapped retinal-pattern photos, examined pore-patterns, listened, prodded, thumped, auscultated. He motioned Jeff back onto the chair and started going over him with a rubber hammer, tapping him sharply in dozens of areas, eliciting a most disconcerting variety of muscular jerks and twitches. Then the hammer was replaced by a small electrode, with which the doctor probed and tested, bringing spasmodic jerks to the muscles of Jeff's back and arms and thighs. Finally, Dr. Gabriel relaxed, sat Jeff down in a soft chair and retired to a small portable instrument cabinet nearby.

Dr. Schiml put out his smoke and stood up. "Any questions before we begin?"

Jeff almost sighed aloud. Any questions? His nerves tingled all over and his mind was full of conjecture--wild, ridiculous guesses of what they would discover in the testing, of what the results would bring. Suppose they learned about the dice? Suppose they found out that he was a fraud, that he was in the Center on a private mission, a mission of death all his own, and no party to their own missions of death? And yet, if he had to follow through, the kind of work he would be assigned to would depend upon the results of the tests—that seemed sure. But what if they rendered him unconscious, knocked him out, used drugs?

His mind raced frantically, searching for some way of stalling things, some way of slowing down the red tape of testing and assignment, to give him time to complete his own mission and get out. But he knew that already he must have aroused suspicions. Schiml must have suspected that all the cards were not on the table, yet Schiml seemed willing to overlook his suspicions. And the wheels had begun to move more and more swiftly, carrying him to the critical point where he would have to sign a release and take an assignment, or reveal his real purpose for being in the Center. If he were to find Conroe, he must find him before the chips were down.

He stared at Schiml, his mind still groping for something to hang onto. He found nothing. "No. No questions, I guess," he said.

The doctor looked at him closely, then shrugged in resignation. "All right," he said, tiredly. "You'll have a whole series of tests of all kinds: physical stamina, mental alertness, reaction time, intelligence, sanity—everything we could possibly need to know. But I should warn you of one thing."

He looked at Jeff, his eyes deadly serious. "All of these future tests are subjective. All of them will tell us about you as a person: how you think, how you behave. Desperately essential stuff, if you're to survive the sort of work we do here. What we find is the whole basis of our assignments."

He paused for a long moment. "You'd be wise to stick to the truth. No embellishments, no fancy stuff. We can't do anything about it if you don't choose to take the advice. But if you falsify, you're tampering with your own life expectancy here."

Jeff blinked, shifting in his seat uneasily. *Don't worry about that, Jack*, he thought. *I won't be around long enough for it to make any difference.* Nevertheless the doctor's words were far from soothing. If only Jeff could maintain the fraud throughout the testing, keep his wits about him as the tests progressed. Then he could get back to the hunt as soon as they were through.

He watched the doctor prepare a long paper on the desk. Then the rapid-fire series of questions began: family history, personal history, history of family disease and personal illness. The questions were swift and businesslike, and Jeff felt his muscles relaxing as he sat back. He answered almost automatically. Then: "Ever been hypnotized before?"

Something in Jeff's mind froze, screaming a warning. "No," he snapped.

Schiml's eyes widened imperceptibly. "Part of the testing should be done under hypnosis, for your sake, and for the sake of speed." His eyes caught Jeff's hard. "Unless you have some reason for objecting—"

"It won't work," Jeff lied swiftly, his mind racing. "Psychic block of some kind—induced in childhood, probably. My father had a block against it too." Every muscle in his body was tense, and he sat forward in his seat, his eyes wide.

Schiml shrugged. "It would make the testing a hundred percent easier on you if you'd allow it. Some of these tests are pretty exhausting and some take a powerful long time without hypnotic-recovery aid. And of course we keep all information strictly confidential—"

"No dice," said Jeff hoarsely.

The doctor shrugged again, glancing over at Dr. Gabriel. "Hear that, Gabe?"

The little doctor shrugged. "His funeral," he growled. He rolled a small, shiny-paneled instrument with earphones to Jeff's side. "We'll start on the less strenuous ones, then. This is a hearing test. Very simple. You just listen, mark down the signals you hear. Keep your eyes on the eyepiece; it records visio-audio correlation times, tells us how soon after you hear a word you form a visual image of it." He snapped the earphones over Jeff's head and moved a printed answer sheet in front of him on the desk. And then the earphones started talking.

There was a long series of words, gradually becoming softer and softer. Jeff marked them down, swiftly, gradually forgetting his surroundings, throwing his attention toward the test. The doctors retired to the other side of the room. They talked to each other in low whispers, until he no longer heard them. There was only the low, insistent whispering in the earphones.

And then the words seemed to grow louder again, but somehow he had lost track of what they meant. He listened, his eyes watching the cool gray pearly screen in the eyepieces. His fingers were poised to write down the words, but he couldn't quite understand the syllables.

They were *nonsense syllables*, syllables with no meaning. His eyes opened wide, a bolt of suspicion shooting through him, and his hands gripped the arms of the chair as he began to rise.

And then the light exploded in his eyes with such agonizing brilliance that it sent shooting pain searing through his brain. He let out a stifled cry. He struggled and tried to rise from the chair. But he was blinded by the piercing beam. And then he felt the needle bite his arm, and the nonsense words in his ears straightened out into meaningful phrases. A soft, soothing voice was saying: "Relax... relax... sit back and relax... relax and rest..."

Slowly the warmth crept over his body, and he felt his muscles relax, even as the voice instructed. He eased gently back into the chair, and soon his mind was clear of fear and worry and suspicion. He was still, sleeping with the peaceful ease of a newborn child.

CHAPTER EIGHT

IT COULD never have been done without hypnosis. Within broad limits, the human body is capable of doing just exactly whatever it thinks it is capable of. But the human body could hardly be blamed if convention had long since decided that exertion was bad, that straining to the limit of endurance was unhealthy, that approaching—even obliquely—the margin of safety of human resiliency was equivalent to approaching death with arms extended. That convention had so declared was well known to the researchers at the Hoffman Center.

But it was also known that the human body under the soothing suggestion of hypnosis could be carried up to that margin of safety and beyond. Indeed, it could be carried almost to the actual breaking point without stir, without a flicker of protest, without a sign of fear.

And these were the conditions that were critically needed in testing for the Mercy Men. Yet, though hypnosis was necessary, the men who came to the Mercy Men without fail rejected hypnosis. Always they held the fear of divulging some secret of their past. Whether because of distrust of the doctors and the testing in the Center, or plain, ordinary malignance of character—no one knew all the motives. But those who needed hypnosis the most rejected it the most vehemently. This forced the development of techniques of hypnosis-by-force.

It would have annoyed Jeff, if he had known. Indeed, it would have driven him to the heights of anger, for Jeff, among other things, was afraid. But he need not have been, and it made little difference that he was. Now Jeff was not suffering from his fear. His mind was in a quiet, happy haze, and he felt his body half-lifted, half-led across the room to the first section of the testing room.

Even now there was a tiny, sharp-voiced sentinel hiding away in a corner of his mind, screaming out its message of alertness and fear to Jeff. But he laughed to himself, sinking deeper into the peacefulness of his walking slumber. Dr. Gabriel's voice was in his ear, his voice smooth and soothing, talking to him quietly, giving simple instructions. Quickly, he took him through the paces of a testing series that would have taken long, hard days to complete. It would have left him in psychotic break at the end, if he had not had the recuperative buffer of hypnosis to help him.

First, he was dressed in soft flannel clothing and moved into the gymnasium. Recorders were attached to his legs and arms and throat. Then he was formally introduced to the treadmill and quietly asked to run it until he collapsed. He smiled and obliged, running as though the furies were at his heels. He ran until his face went purple and his muscles knotted. At last he fell down, unable to continue.

This happened after ten minutes of top-limit running. Then came five minutes of recuperation under suggestion: "Your heart is beating slower. You're breathing slowly and deeply... relaxing... relaxing." Someone took his arm and he was off again, this time on the old, reliable Harvard Step-Test, jumping up on the chair and back down. He did this until once again he lay panting on the floor, hardly able to move as his pulse and respiration changes were carefully recorded.

Next in line came a lively handball game. He was handed a small, hard rubber ball, and asked to engage in a game of catch with a machine that was stationed at the end of a cubby. The machine played hard, spinning the ball around and hurling it at Jeff with such incredible rapidity that he was forced to abandon all thinking. Instinctively, he reached out to catch the ball. His fingers burned with pain as he caught it and passed it in, only to have it hurled back out again, twice as fast. Soon he moved as automatically as a machine, catching, hurling, his mind refusing to accept the aching and swelling in his fingers, as the ball struck and struck and struck...

Then a small ladder was rolled in. He listened carefully to instructions and then ran up and down the ladder until he collapsed off the top. He was rested gently on the floor while blood samples were taken from his arm. Then he sat, staring dully at the floor. A voice said, "Relax, Jeff, take a rest. Sleep quietly, Jeff. You'll be ready to dig in and fight in a minute. Now just relax."

Several people were about; one brought him a heavy, sugary drink, lukewarm and revolting. He drank it, gagging, spilling it all down his shirtfront. Then he grinned and licked his lips while further blood samples were drawn. And then, he was allowed to take a drink of cool water. He was left staring at his feet for five whole minutes of recuperation before the next stage of the testing commenced.

The lights were in three long columns. They extended as

far as Jeff could see to the horizon. Some were blinking; some shone with steady intensity, while others were dark.

"Call the columns one, two and three," said Dr. Gabriel, close by, his voice soft with patience. "Record the position of the lights as you see them now. Then when the signal sounds, start recording every light change you see in all three columns. Do it fast, Jeff, as fast as you can."

The eye is a wonderful instrument of precision, capable of detecting an infinitude of movement and change. It is delicate enough to distinguish, if necessary, each and every still frame composing the motion picture that flickers so swiftly before it on the white screen. Jeff's fingers moved, his pencil recorded, quickly moving from column one to column two, and on to column three. The pencil moved swiftly until the test was over.

Then on to the next test...

Electrode leads were fastened to each of his ten toes and each of his ten fingers.

"Listen once, Jeff. Right first toe corresponds to left thumb; right second toe to right index finger. (Wonderful stuff, hypno-palamine, only one repetition to learn) When you feel a shock in a toe, press the button for the corresponding finger. Ready now, Jeff, as fast as you can."

Shock, press, shock, press. Jeff's mind was still, silent, a blank, an open circuit for reactions to speed through without hindrance, without modulation. Another round done and on to the next...

Doctor Schiml's pale face loomed up from some distant place. "Everything all right?"

"Going fine, fine. Smooth as can be."

"No snags anywhere?"

"No, no snags. None that I can see—yet."

"I want a smoke."

Dr. Gabriel relaxed, offered Jeff a smoke from a crumpled

pack, extended his lighter and smiled. He noticed that Jeff's wide eyes missed their focus, could not see the extended flame: "How do you feel, Jeff?"

"Fine, fine—"

"Still got a lot to do."

A flicker of fear crossed the dull eyes. "Fine. Only I hope..."

"Yes?"

" ...hope we finish. I'm tired."

"Sleepy?"

"Yeah, sleepy."

"Well, we'll have everything on punched cards for Tilly in a couple of hours or so. All the factors about you that this testing will unearth would take a research staff five hundred years to integrate down to the point where it would mean anything. With Tilly it takes five minutes. She doesn't make mistakes, either."

"Nice Tilly."

"And after the results come through, you're assigned and you sign your release and you're on your way to money."

Again the flicker of fear came, deeper this time. "Money..."

More tests, more tests. Hear a sound, punch a button. See a picture, record it. Test after endless test, dozens of records, his brain growing tired, tired. Then into the bright, gleaming room, up onto the green-draped table.

"No pain, Jeff, nothing to worry about. Be over in just a minute."

His eyes caught the slender, wicked-looking trefine; he heard the buzz of the motor, felt the grinding shock. But there was no reaction, no pain. And then he felt a curious tingling in his arms and legs, as the small electroencephalograph end plates entered his skull through the tiny drilled holes.

He watched with dull eyes as the little lights on the control board nearby began blinking on and off, on and off. The flashes followed a hectic, nervous pattern, registering individual brain-cell activity onto supersensitive stroboscopic film. This, in turn, was fed down automatically to Tilly for analysis. And then the trefine holes were plugged up again and his head was tightly taped, and he was moved back into another room for another five-minute recovery.

"Hit the ink blots yet?"

"Not yet, Rog. Take it easy, we're coming along. Ink blots and intelligence runs next, and so on."

Something stirred deep in Jeff's mind, even through the soothing delusions of hypnosis. It stirred and cried out at the first sign of the strange, colored forms on the cards. Something deep in Jeff's mind forced its way out to his lips as Dr. Gabriel said softly, "Just look at them, Jeff, and tell me what you see."

"No! Take them away."

"What's that? Gently, Jeff. Relax and take a look."

Jeff was on his feet, backing away, a wild, helpless, cornered fire in his eyes. "Take them away. Get me out of here. Go away—"

"Jeff!" The voice was sharp, commanding. "Sit down, Jeff."

Jeff sank down in the seat, gingerly, eyes wary. The doctor moved his hand and Jeff jumped a foot, his teeth chattering.

"What's the matter, Jeff?"

"I—I don't like...those...cards."

"But they're only ink blots, Jeff."

Jeff frowned and squinted at the cards. He scratched his head in perplexity. Slowly he sank back down in the chair, didn't even notice as the web-belt restrainers closed over his arms and legs, tightened down.

"Now look at the pictures, Jeff. Tell me what you see."

The perplexity grew on his heavy face, but he looked and talked, slowly, hoarsely. A dog's head, a little gnome, a big red bat.

"Gently, Jeff. Nothing to be afraid of. Relax, man, relax…"

Then came the word-association tests: half an hour of words and answers, while fear curled up through Jeff's brain, gathering, crouching, ready to spring, waiting in horrible anticipation for something, something that was coming as sure as hour followed hour. Jeff felt the web restrainers cutting his wrists, as the words were read. He trembled in growing foreboding.

Dr. Schiml's face was back, still concerned, his eyes bright. "Going all right, Gabe?"

"Dunno, Rog. Something funny with the ink blots. You can glance at the report. Word association all screwed up too. Can't spot it, but there's something funny."

"Give him a minute's rest and reinforce the palamine. Probably got a powerful vitality opposing it."

Dr. Gabriel was back in a moment, and another needle nibbled Jeff's arm briefly. Then the doctor walked to the desk, took out the small, square plastic box. He dropped the cards out into his hand. They were plain-backed little cards with bright red symbols on their faces.

Dr. Gabriel held them under Jeff's nose. "Rhine cards," he said softly. "Four different symbols, Jeff. Look close. A square, a circle…"

It was like a gouge, jammed down through Jeff's mind, ripping it without mercy. A red-hot, steaming poker was being rammed into the soft, waxy tissue of his brain.

"My God, hold him!"

Jeff screamed, wide awake, his eyes bulging with terror. With an animal-like roar he wrenched at his restrainers,

162

ripped them out of the raw wood and plunged across the room in blind, terrified flight. He ran across the room and struck the solid brick wall full face. He hit with a sickening thud, pounded at the wall with his fists, screaming out again and again. And then he collapsed to the floor, his nose broken, his face bleeding, his fingers raw with the nails broken.

And as he slid into merciful unconsciousness, they heard him blubbering: "He killed my father...killed him killed him...killed him...killed him..."

Hours later he stirred. He almost screamed out in pain as he tried to move his arm. His chest burned as he breathed. When he opened his eyes, an almost unbearable, pounding ache struck down through his skull. He recognized his room, saw the empty bed across from him. Then he raised an arm, felt the bandaging around his face, his neck.

He listened fearfully and his ears caught only the harsh, gurgling breathing of the man in the next room: the man called Tinker, whose doom as a Mercy Man had not been quite sealed, who breathed on, shallowly, breaking the deadly silence.

What had happened?

Jeff sat bolt upright in the darkness, ignoring the stabbing pain that shot through his chest and neck. What had happened? Why was he bandaged? What was the meaning of the pure, naked, paralyzing fear that was gripping him like a vise? He stared through the darkness at the opposite bed, and blinked. What had happened...what...what?

Of course. He had been in the file room. He'd been caught. Schiml had caught him and he had been taken down for testing. And then: *a bright light, nonsense words in his ear, a needle...*

Gasping with pain, Jeff rolled out of bed, searched

underneath for his shoes. With an audible sob, he retrieved the crumpled card from under the inner sole. Then they hadn't gotten the card. They didn't know. But what could have happened? Slowly, other things came back: there had been a scream; he had felt a shock, as though molten lead had been sent streaming through his veins, and then he had struck the wall like a ten-ton truck.

He groped for his watch, stared at it, hardly believing his eyes. It read seven P.M. It had been almost one A.M. when they had taken him down to Dr. Gabriel. It couldn't be seven in the evening again. Unless he had slept around the clock. He listened to the watch; it was still running. Whatever had happened had thrown him, thrown him so hard that he had slept for almost twenty-four hours. And in the course of that time...

The horrible loss struck him suddenly, worming its way through to open realization. Twenty-four hours later—a day gone, a whole day for Conroe to use to move deeper into hiding. He sank back on the bed and groaned, despair heavy in his mind. A day gone, a precious day. Somewhere the man was in the Center. But to locate him now, after he had had such time—how could Jeff do it?

He felt a greater urgency now. No matter what they had found in the testing, he had no time left to hunt. The next step on this one-way road was assignment and the signing of a release—the point of no return.

And through it all, something ate at his mind: some curious question, some phantom he could not pin down, a shadow figure which loomed up again and again in his mind, haunting him—the shadow of fearful doubt. Why the shock? Why had he broken loose? What had driven him to punish his arms and legs so mercilessly on the restrainers? What monstrous demon had torn loose in his mind? What gaping sore had the doctors scraped over to drive him to such extremes of fear and horror? *And why was the same feeling there in his mind whenever he thought of Paul Conroe?*

He sighed. He needed help and he knew it. He needed help desperately. Here, in a whirlpool of hatred and selfishness, he needed help more than he had ever needed it, help to track down this phantom shadow, help to corner it, to kill it. And the only ones he could ask for help were those around him, the Mercy Men themselves. He needed their help, if only to escape becoming one of them.

He dozed, then woke a little later and listened. There was an air of tension in the room, a whisper of something gone wrong. Jeff forced himself up on his elbow, tried to peer through the darkness. Something had happened just before he awoke. He listened to the deathly stillness in the room.

And then he knew what it was. The breathing in the next room had stopped.

He lay back, his heart pounding, listening to the rasping of his own breath, fear and despair rising to new heights in his mind. Death had come, then. One man who would never see the payoff he so eagerly awaited. Jeff had felt death pass over the room, and he knew, instinctively, that the unit would know it too without a single word passing from a single mouth. The sense of death was a tangible thing here, moving with silent, imponderable footfalls from room to room.

For the first time, Jeff felt a kinship, a depth of understanding to share with the Mercy Men. And there was a depth of fear, deep down, which he knew now that he must share with them too. Painfully, he rolled over on his side and stared into the darkness for long minutes before he fell into fitful sleep.

CHAPTER NINE

A VOICE was talking across the room, a muffled, mysterious rumble of up-and-down sounds. Slowly Jeff dragged his mind out of the clinging depths of nightmare, back to the stuffy, dimly lit room. How long had he slept? And how late was it now? The soft voices across the room gave no clue, and his aching mind was too tired to care any more. He just lay in the dim light, every muscle aching, his mind returning again and again to the nightmare he had been reliving for the thousandth time.

It had been horribly sharp this time, clear as noonday: the same subject as always, the same face, the same horrible knowledge, and the same soul-wrenching hatred welling up and bubbling over in his mind. Always it was hatred without plan or form, pure, disorganized animal fury. But this time the dream had been more coherent, clearer, more unmistakable and vicious.

He had been walking down the street in the heart of the city. Yes, it was mid-morning. The sun's heat was unbearable already, and his jacket and shirt were damp. What was he doing that morning? Was he on his way to the survey depot with some information on the next Mars run? It didn't really matter. But he turned into the building and then it hit him.

It was like the shock that had struck him in the testing room, he thought. He had run into the man bodily. Stepping back to beg his pardon, he saw the man's face. That's where the dream went wild, just as his mind had gone wild on that sunny morning so long ago. He saw the man turn and run like the wind, snaking into the flowing stream of people on the street. Jeff followed, shouting, his fists and legs churning through the masses of people. He screamed in hoarse, maddened despair as he saw the figure vanish before his eyes.

And then he was leaning against the wall, panting, tears streaming down his face. Unable to understand, knowing only that this was the man whose face had haunted his dreams all his life, he acknowledged this was the man he would have to kill.

His eyes snapped open. The voices across the room were louder. Jeff listened. One voice was a woman's—Blackie's, of course. There was no mistaking the Nasty Frenchman's nasal twang. But the third voice— Jeff blinked his eyes. He moved his head to see the little group across the room.

They were huddled around a small infrared coffee maker: Blackie, the Nasty Frenchman, and the huge, bald-headed man called Harpo. Blackie's voice was sharp and pleading as she echoed the Nasty Frenchman in angry protest. Harpo's heavy bass rumbled an undertone to the whispered discussion. Painfully, Jeff drew himself up on an elbow and turned his ear in the direction of the huddle, as the words drifted to him, unclearly:

"I say find out who and do something about it," the Nasty Frenchman was insisting angrily. His face was red and spiteful, and his eyes flashed as he glared up at Harpo. "We're out of it completely. Don't you see that? Because of this switch, we're off the payroll—ditched like common scum! Well, the job I've been on was to pay two hundred thousand dollars, with practically no risk involved. And I'll kill the man that's cutting me out of it."

Harpo's voice was soothing. "So maybe you're daydreaming. Maybe there won't be any switch of jobs at all."

"I saw the report, I tell you. It was signed by Schiml himself."

Harpo looked up sharply. "You actually saw Schiml's signature on it?"

"I saw it. I'm taken off assignment and so are you. We're

both shoved out. Can't you get that straight? After all this time—and just because they get somebody in here that gets them excited."

Harpo snorted. "So they've gone off on these spook hunts before. Where do you think it'll take them this time? Extrasensory powers!" The huge man spat in disdain. "Have you ever seen anybody with extra-sensory powers? Well, neither have I. Look, Jacques, let's face it: Schiml would give his left arm at the shoulder to have proof of extra-sensory powers in any form." Harpo grinned unpleasantly. "You've seen proof of that before. He believes in it, he wants to prove it. And every now and then he's going to have a try at it just to keep himself happy, just to keep in form. There's no call to get excited."

"But he's got a solid prospect this time," Blackie snapped. "From the stories I've heard the guy is a phenomenon. Hit top scores on the cards—highest they've ever recorded here. Other things too, like peeling the paper off the walls just by looking at them, or closing up opened wounds in ten minutes.

"So you hear stories! Around here I don't believe anything I hear." Harpo shifted uneasily. "If there was anything tangible, anything we could put our hands on, I'd listen. But there's not—no proof, no nothing but a lot of wild stories. And I've even heard better stories in my time. You can't go around fighting stories—"

Jeff sat bolt upright, something shouting out in his brain. He grabbed for his shoes, oblivious to the agonizing pain in his muscles, fumbled eagerly, his mind screaming in excitement. "What kind of proof do you want?" he growled.

Harpo stared up at him, as though seeing a ghost. "You awake!" he gasped. And then: "Any kind of proof!"

"Then take a look at this." And Jeff tossed the crumpled card down in the middle of the huddle.

Blackie was on her feet, her eyes eager. "Didn't know you were anywhere near ready to wake up," she said. "You look like they really gave you the works."

"Well, something happened, all right. I don't know whether I'm coming or going."

Blackie nodded. "You never do, after testing. They came here for you, and I told them you'd gone out for a stroll. But I guess they found you." She put a cup of coffee in Jeff's hand and motioned toward the card. "You got that out of the file without being spotted?"

Jeff's eyes met hers for the briefest instant. "That's right. And I heard what you were talking about." He caught the little note of warning in her eyes: the silent, helpless appeal. He shook his head imperceptibly. He knew then that she hadn't told the others about their battle over the dice. He pointed to the card. "I think that answers a lot of things."

Harpo's eyes were suspicious. "How do you know that's the man?"

"Because I drove him in here, that's why." Jeff's voice was a snarl; it sounded sharp in the quiet room. "I knew he was here because he came here to escape me. But I didn't know he had any connection with ESP until I saw the card."

Harpo stared at the card, then at Jeff. "You mean you drove him in here?"

"That's right. Because I'd have killed him if he didn't come." Jeff's face was dark as he turned to the girl. "Tell him, Blackie. Tell him why I'm here."

Blackie told them. They listened with widening eyes, and the room was still as a tomb.

"And you came in here to kill this man—nothing more?" Harpo's voice was incredulous. "But man, you're on thin ice, very thin ice. If they tested you last night, you'll be assigned. Why, you could be forced to sign a release any time."

"I know it, I know it. Can't you see why there isn't time

to bicker now?" Jeff's voice cracked in the still room, sharp and urgent. "This is the man, the one I'm looking for and the one you're looking for, the one with ESP that's got Schiml and his men so excited! It's here on the card!"

Harpo's eyes were narrow. "Any other proof besides the card that Conroe is the man?"

Jeff's voice was low with hate. "Look. I've been hunting the man down for five years. A long time. I've hunted him wherever he's gone. I've had the best detective agency in North America working with me hand and foot, tracking him down. But they haven't caught him. We've almost caught him, we've haunted him, we've run him back and forth across the country and world until he's ragged. But we've never caught him. Isn't there some significance to that? Time and again we've come so close that we couldn't miss—and then we missed. We've come too close too many times for coincidence. There's another factor, a factor that's giving Conroe warning, time after time. It's allowed him to slip out of perfectly sealed traps—*a factor like precognition, for instance.*"

There was a long silence. Then the Nasty Frenchman was on his feet, his lips stretched in a malicious grin. "If we move fast enough, we can stop it—cut it off at the bud. We're off the payroll now. But we can get back on it again, if their boy wonder dies."

Harpo's eyes flashed. "And how do you plan to do it?"

"Nothing simpler in the world. We just find the guy." The Nasty Frenchman's grin widened. "Then after we find him, we tell our friend Jeff about it. Nothing more. Jeff'll take it from there. Right, Jeff?"

Jeff's heart pounded against his ribs. "That's right," he said, his voice hoarse with eagerness. "Just find him for me."

Harpo bent over slowly, poured another cup of coffee. "Then let's talk plans," he said softly.

The planning went smoothly. Jeff sat forward eagerly. The despair and hopelessness of an hour before evaporated, leaving fingers of wild excitement creeping through his muscles, up and down his spine. These people knew where they were; they knew how to hunt in this evil place, where to go, what to do. This was the help he needed to complete his mission, the help he'd needed from the start. And now, at last, nothing would go wrong. Carefully, the last trap was laid—the final drive in this manhunt that had lasted so long and been so fruitless. This time there would be no slip.

Harpo fingered the card thoughtfully. "These dates must have some significance. Were there any signs of Conroe's visits here at those times?"

Jeff shook his head. "No sign. He couldn't have been here for more than three days at a time, or I'd have known about it."

Harpo grunted, his eyes sharp on Jeff's face. "And you had no definite, direct evidence that he was somehow using an extra-sensory talent in eluding you?"

Jeff scowled. "No direct evidence. I'm afraid not. There was no reason to suspect it, until I found the card. Then hindsight started filling in funny things that had gone un-noticed before."

Harpo nodded. "Yes. That's the way it would be. But Schiml must have had direct enough evidence. This ESP study is just like space travel was. They've been after it for years; they start after it time after time, every time a new angle comes up. Because if they succeed it could mean so much to so many people."

The Nasty Frenchman snorted. "Sure. Like running us out of paying jobs for good and all, after all the risks we've taken. Open the door to ESP for them, and there wouldn't be any other work in the Center for twenty years. And if we don't happen to be what they're looking for—" He ran his finger across his throat and scowled. "The man is here. We've got to have information on him, past and present. That means we'll have to search the Archives. There's no better approach." He turned his sharp little eyes on Jeff. "You know how the electronic files work. You're the one that can dig out what we need to know in the Archives."

Jeff nodded. "But I'll need time to work without interruption. Can you get me into the Archive files without being caught?"

The Nasty Frenchman nodded eagerly. "Nothing to it. Give us half an hour to clear the way and get the guards taken care of." He glanced up at Harpo. "The old fire-alarm gag should do it, all right. Then you can walk right down."

"And can you keep it clear for me, say, for an hour or so?"

"For five hours, if necessary." Harpo stood up sharply. "We'll start now to get things lined up. When it's clear, I'll give you a flicker on the phone. Don't answer it. Just come along. Blackie can draw you a map while you wait." The bald-headed giant started to leave, then turned back. "And don't let any alarm bells disturb you. We've found ways of occupying guards before." He touched his forehead briefly, and he and the Nasty Frenchman disappeared into the corridor.

"I think it'll work," Jeff breathed, tucking Blackie's crude penciled map into his pocket. "I think we've got him. Once we know where he is and what they're going to do with him—" He grinned up at her, his eyes shining. "His time's running out, Blackie. He's as good as dead."

The girl leaned forward, pouring coffee, sitting silently. Jeff watched her face, as if seeing it for the first time. Indeed, for the first time, the girl's face seemed softer. In the dim light of the room, the hard lines melted away, magically. Her face appeared younger and fresher, as though some curious mask had dropped away in the course of the evening.

But her eyes were troubled as she watched Jeff and lifted her coffee cup in mock salute. "To the Hunter," she said softly.

Jeff raised his own cup. "Yes. But not for long now."

"It can't go on much longer, Jeff. Your number's up next."

"For assignment?" Jeff's eyes flashed. "Do you think that makes any difference to me? I'm following through to the end on this, no matter what happens."

"But, Jeff, you can't sign a release."

Jeff stared at her in the silent room. "Why not? If it's the only thing I can do——"

Her eyes were wide and very dark. "Oh, Jeff, you're in terrible danger here."

"I know that."

"You don't, you don't." The girl was shaking her head, tears rising to her eyes. "You don't know anything, Jeff, about the Mercy Men or the kind of work they do. Oh, I know, you think you do. But you don't, really. Look, Jeff—look at it straight—you're young, you're smart. There are other ways to spend your life, more important things for you to do. Can't you see that? No man is worth throwing your life away for, no matter what he's done to you. That's what you're doing. You're walking down a blind alley, into a death trap! Get out, while you can."

Jeff's head was shaking, his lips tight, until the color fled them, leaving pale gray lines. "I can't get out. I just can't. Nothing anyone could say could drive me out now."

"But you've got to run while you can! Oh, yes, go down there tonight if you must, try to find him. But if you don't find him, cut and run. Jeff, get out, tonight. They can't stop you; they have no legal hold on you, yet. But once they bring in a release, you're hooked. It'll be too late then."

Jeff's eyes narrowed, and he sat down on the bed and

faced the girl. There was an elfin expression on her face, a curious intensity in her large gray eyes that he had never seen before. "What do you care?" he asked suddenly. "What do you care what I do?"

The girl's voice was low, and the words tumbled out so rapidly that he could hardly follow them. "Look, Jeff, you and me—we could work as a team. Don't you see what we could do? We could get out of here, together. We could get out of the city, go to the West Coast. The dice, think of the dice, man—we could clean up! You don't belong in here on the rack for slaughter. And I wouldn't belong here, either, if we could work together—"

Somewhere in the distance an alarm bell began ringing, insistently, clang-clanging down the corridors. Then there was a rush of feet, shouted orders and calls up and down the hallway, and the squeak of three jitneys passing by in rapid succession. Then, abruptly, the corridor fell silent again.

Jeff hardly noticed the clamor. He stared at the girl, his hands trembling. "Blackie, Blackie, think what you're saying. The tough-luck jinx. Have you forgotten? You're safe from it here. But outside, what would happen? We might make a go of it, yes, but what if the jinx followed us?"

"Oh, but Jeff, that's silly." She swallowed, her eyes almost overflowing as she tried to blink back the tears. "It isn't just selfishness, Jeff. I could stay here. I talked to Schiml this afternoon, before Harpo and Jacques started talking. They're out—yes. But I'm not. He wants me to stay, says there's a place for me in the work. But I don't want to stay."

Jeff was shaking his head slowly, his eyes tired. "It's no dice, Blackie. Not now. After I get Conroe, after I get out of here, then maybe I could think about it. But I haven't given this dice business any thought at all. Can't you see? I'd have to think it out, carefully, all its ramifications. And I haven't been able to do that. It hasn't mattered enough. I've got a man to kill, first, before anything else. And I'm going to kill him. I'm going to kill him tonight."

"Then do it for sure. Get him tonight! And then get out, before something happens—"

In the corner the phone gave two sharp rings, then lapsed into silence. Their eyes met, sharply, desperately. "Nothing's going to happen," Jeff said softly. "Don't worry about it. I've been at this too long for anything to happen."

There was a frantic light in the girl's gray eyes as she looked up at him, a depth and sincerity he had never seen before. Her eyes pleaded with him. "You don't know, you don't know…"

And then they were in each other's arms, drawing each other close, desperately. His hard lips met her soft ones, met and held. Then when they parted there was another look in her eyes, and he heard her breath cut sharply by his ear. "Jeff—"

Gently he put a finger to his lips, loosened her arms from around him. "Don't say it," he whispered. "Not now, Blackie. Not now—"

And then he was outside, in the corridor. The cool air caught him and he ran down the corridor toward the stairs. He hurried against the time the men had prepared for his safety. And as he ran, he felt his heart pounding in his ears, and he knew the hour was drawing close.

CHAPTER TEN

JACQUES and Harpo were waiting for him at the head of the escalator. He nodded and followed them down the corridor to the small jitney car that was waiting.

"All set?"

"All set. The guards are all busy up in N unit putting out a fire. They won't be down to bother us for a couple of hours." The Nasty Frenchman scowled disdainfully. "But you'll have to hurry. When they come back, we'll have a time stalling them again."

Jeff nodded. "That should be enough. Then maybe we'll have other things to occupy the guards tonight."

The jitney started with a lurch and a squawk. Harpo handled the controls, running the little car swiftly down the corridor. It swung suddenly into a pitch-black tunnel, took an abrupt dip and began to spiral downward at a wild rate. Jeff grabbed the handrail and gasped.

"It's a long way down," Harpo chuckled, sitting back in the darkness. "The Archives hold the permanent records of the entire Hoffman Center since it was first opened. That's why it's a vault, so that bombing won't destroy it. It's one of the most valuable tombs in history."

The jitney shot out into a lighted corridor. Jeff swallowed and felt his ears pop. The little car whizzed through a maze of tunnels and corridors. Finally it settled down to the floor before the heavy steel doors at the end of a large corridor.

Without a word, Harpo moved down to the end of the corridor, and drew the jitney car with him. He opened the motor hood, started pawing around busily inside.

The Nasty Frenchman chuckled. "If anyone wanders by, that jitney alarm siren goes off, and Harpo's just a poor technician trying to make it stop." The little man walked quickly to the steel doors. "It's not the first time I've had to work on these," he said slyly. "We wanted in here a few months ago, when they were trying to pull a shakedown deal on some of us. I worked out the combination pattern then; it took me three days. They change the combination periodically, of course, but the pattern is built into the lock."

He opened a small leather case and placed an instrument up against the lock. A long, thin wire was poised and ready in his other hand. Jeff heard several muffled clicks; then Jacques inserted the wire sharply into something. An alarm bell above the door gave one dull, half-hearted clunk and relapsed into silence, as though changing its mind at the last moment. A moment later the little Frenchman looked up and winked, and the steel vault door rolled slowly back.

The place smelled damp and empty. Three walls and half of the fourth were occupied with electronic file controls. The bulk of the room was taken up with tables, microviewers, readers, recorders, and other study-apparatus. There was nothing small in the room; the whole place breathed of bigness, of complexity, of many years of work and wisdom, of many lives and many, many deaths. It was a record-room that many lives had built.

Jeff moved in toward the control panel. He located the master coder and sat down in a chair before it, his eyes running over it carefully, sizing up the mammoth filing machine. And then, quite suddenly, he felt terribly afraid. A knot grew in his stomach and a cold sweat broke out on his forehead. A face was again looming up sharply in his mind. It was the huge, ghoulish face that had come to him again and again in his dreams; the face full of hatred and viciousness—pale and inhuman.

It was the face of a heartless, pointless, bloody assassin. But was that all? Or was there more to that face, more to that dream than Jeff had ever suspected? Something deep in his mind stirred, sending a chill down his spine. His hand trembled as he ran a hand over the control panel. A ghost was there at his elbow, a ghost that had followed him on this nebulous trail of bitterness and hatred for so long—a trail that would end in this very room.

He shook his head angrily. There was no time for panic, no time for ruminating. He picked the panel-code combination for the Mercy Men and the research unit. Then he computed the coding for Conroe's name. With trembling fingers, he typed out the coding, punched the tracer button and sat back, his heart thumping wildly. He watched the receiver slot for the telltale file cards and folio.

The file squeaked and chattered and whirred and moaned, and finally the pale instruction panel lighted up: No Information.

Jeff blinked, a chill running up his back. These files were the final appeal; the information had to be here. Quickly, he computed a description coding, fed it in and waited again in mounting tension. Still no information. He picked the code card from his pocket, the card from the Mercy Men's file up above, the card with the Hoffman Center's own picture of Conroe on it. He fed it into the photoelectric tracer, marked in the necessary coding for an unlimited file search: "Any person resembling this description in any way: any information on—" Again he sat back, breathing heavily.

The whirring went on and on. Then, inexorably, the little panel flickered and spelled out a single word:

"Unknown."

Jeff choked. He stared at the panel, his whole body shaking, and went through the coding again, step by step, searching for an error, finding none. It was impossible, it couldn't be so—and yet, the files were empty of information. As though there had never been a Paul Conroe. There was not even a reference card to the card in the Mercy Men's files.

He stared at the panel, his mind rebelling in protest. Nothing, not even a trace in the one place where there had to be complete information. He had come to a dead end—the last dead end there could be in the Hoffman Center.

The Nasty Frenchman lit a cigarette and watched Jeff from bright eyes. "No luck?"

"No luck," said Jeff, brokenly. "We're beaten. That's all."

"But there must be—"

"Well, there's not!" Jeff slammed his fist down on the table with a crash, his eyes blazing. "There's not a trace, not a whisper of the man in here. There has to be—and there's not. It's the same as every other time: a blank wall. Blank wall after blank wall. I'm getting tired of them, so miserably tired of running into blind alley after blind alley." He stood up, his shoulders sagging. "I'm too tired of it to keep it up. There's no point to gambling any longer. I'm getting out of here while I've got a whole skin."

"Maybe you've got more time than you think." The Nasty Frenchman eyed him in alarm. "This is no time to run out. It may be weeks before you're assigned."

Jeff stared at him. "Well, I know one way to find out." He walked over to the control panel, stabbed an angry finger at the master coder, picked out the coding for "J. Meyer." "They'll have me here too," he snapped. "The whole works about me: what the testing said, what they're going to do to me. That's one way to find out." Quickly, he typed out the coding, punched the tracer button...

The machinery whirred again, briefly. Then there was a click in the receiver slot and another and another. Jeff blinked at it as the microfilm rolls continued to fall down. Then he reached out to the single white card that fell on top of the rolls. His fingers were damp as he took the card. His own death warrant, perhaps? He glanced at the card and froze. His head began pounding as if it would burst.

"J. Meyer" he had punched in, and that was what the card said—*but not Jeffrey Meyer.* The card held a photo of a middle-aged, gray-haired man, and the typewritten name at the top said: JACOB MEYER.

And the picture was a photograph of his father's face.

It was impossible, incredible, but he stared at the card in his hand. It did not disappear; it stayed there. It still said: "Jacob Meyer"; it still showed the beloved features of his father, staring up at him blankly from the card. *His father!*

His heart pounded as he stared at the brief typewritten notation below the picture: "Born 11 August, 2050, Des Moines, Iowa; married 3 Dec. 2077, wife died childbirth 27 November 2078; one son Jeffrey born 27 November 2078." Then below were a series of dates: date of bachelor's degree, date of Master's and Doctorate; Associate Professor of Statistics at Rutgers University, 2079-2084; joined Government Bureau of Statistics in 2085. Finally, at the bottom of the card were a long series of reference numbers to microfilm files.

Jeff sank down in the chair, his mind spinning helplessly. He turned dazed eyes to the Nasty Frenchman. "You might as well go," he said. "I've got to do some reading."

Feverishly, he scooped up the microfilm rolls, carried them to the nearest reader, twisted the spool into the machine and bent his eyes to the viewing slot, his heart pounding in his throat...

The first roll was a long, detailed series of abstracts of statistical papers, all written by Jacob A. Meyer, Ph.D., all covered with marginal notes in a scrawling, spidery hand and initialed "R. D. S." The papers covered a multitude of studies; some dealt with the very techniques of statistical analyses themselves, others were concerned with specific studies that had been done.

The papers were written in scholarly manner, perfectly well documented, but the marginal notes found fault continually, both with the samplings noted and the conclusions drawn. Jeff read through some of the papers and he scowled. They dated over a period of the four years when his father had been teaching statistics. There were several dozen papers, all with marginal notes, none of which made much sense to Jeff. With a sigh, he pulled out the roll, fed in another.

This one seemed a little more rewarding. It was a letter, signed by Roger D. Schiml, M.D., dated almost twenty years before, addressed to the Government Bureau of Statistics. Jeff's eyes skimmed the letter briefly, catching words here, phrases there: ...as director of research at the Hoffman Center, considered it my duty to bring this unbelievable condition to the attention of higher authorities... Naturally, a statistical analysis must be made of the matter before it can be concluded that there has been a marked increase in mental illness of any kind in the general populace... have followed Dr. Meyer's analyses in the past with much interest, and would be pleased if he could come to the Hoffman Center within the next month to commence such a study...

There was nothing tangible, nothing that made sense. Jeff shuffled through the rolls, popped another into place in the reader. This time he read much more closely a letter from an unknown person to Dr. Schiml. It was dated almost a year later than the former letter. This note referred in several places to the "Almost unbelievable results of the statistical study done several months ago." It also referred to the investigation just concluded of possible disturbing elements in the analysis. The final paragraph Jeff read through three times, his eyes nearly popping.

There was no doubt that the data was sound, and properly collected; naturally, the results of the analysis followed mathematically from the data. It seemed, therefore, that we were dealing with a disturbing factor heretofore quite unsuspected. Our investigation leads us to the inavoidable, though hardly credible, conclusion that Dr. Jacob A. Meyer *was himself* the sole disturbing factor in the analysis. No other possibility fits the facts of the picture. We recommend therefore that an intensive study of Dr. Meyer's previous work be undertaken, with a view to answering the obvious questions aroused by such a report. We also recommend that this be undertaken without delay.

At the very top of the letter, in red letters, was the government's careful restriction: TOP SECRET.

Another roll went into the reader. This held the letterhead of a New York psychiatrist. Jeff's eyes caught the name and he read eagerly:

Dear Dr. Schiml:

We have studied the microfilm records you posted to us with extreme care, and undertaken the study of Jacob Meyer, as instructed. Although it is impossible to make a positive diagnosis without interviewing and examining the patient in person, we are inclined to support your views as stated in your letter. As to the possibility of other more remarkable phenomena occurring, we are not prepared to comment. But we must point out that this man almost certainly undergoes a regular manic-depressive cycle, may be dangerously depressed, even suicidal, in a depressive low, and may endanger himself and others in a manic period of elation. Such a person is extremely dangerous and should not be allowed freedom to go as he chooses.

Jeff looked up, tears streaming from his eyes. His whole body was wet with perspiration. He could hardly keep his balance as he stood up. What lies! The idea that his father could have been insane, that he could have falsified any sort of statistical report that he had done—it was impossible, a pack of incredible lies. But they were here, on the files of the greatest medical center on the face of the earth—lies about his father, lies that Jeff couldn't even attack because he could not understand them.

The door swung open sharply, and the Nasty Frenchman stuck his head in, panting. "Better get going," he snarled. "There are guards coming." His head disappeared abruptly, and Jeff heard Harpo's voice bellow at him: "Come on, we've got to run!"

Jeff's legs would hardly move. He felt numb as though a thousand nerve centers had been suddenly struck all at once. He fumbled, pouring the microfilm rolls into his pockets, his mind whirling. There was no sense to it: no understanding, no explanation. Somehow, he knew, there was a tie-in between these records of his father, taken so long ago, and the absence of any information on Paul Conroe in the files. But he couldn't find the link.

He ran out into the hall, leaped into the jitney car. He hung on for dear life as it sped up through the tunnel, into the blackness of the spiral once again. Suddenly, in his ears, another sound exploded, the loud, insistent clang of an alarm bell.

Harpo looked at the Nasty Frenchman and then at Jeff. "Oh, oh," he said softly. "They're onto something; that's a general muster. We'd better get back to quarters—and fast!"

He shoved the controls ahead a bit further, and Jeff felt the car leap ahead. Finally it settled down in the quarters corridor. They leaped out, Harpo set the dials for the car to return, and the three men ran for their quarters, the bell still clanging in their ears.

In Jeff's mind thoughts were tumbling as he ran—hopeless thoughts, uneasy thoughts. As he had ridden up, little chinks had fallen into place in his mind. Little spaces that he had never understood suddenly began to make sense, adding up to questions, big questions. It was too pat, too easy that Conroe should come in here and vanish as if he had never been alive. Things didn't happen that way, not even for Conroe.

Other things came into focus, slowly, flickering briefly through his mind—things that had happened years before, things that seemed, suddenly, to mean something. Then, just as they came into focus, they flickered back out of reach again. They were incidents like the night in the gambling room; like the night in the nightclub with the dancer swaying before him; like the sudden, shocking jolt that had awakened him from the depths of hypnosis and driven him face-first into a stone wall; things like the curious viciousness of his hatred for Paul Conroe—a hate that had carried him to the ends of the earth. But now that hate lay stalemated, and new and more frightening information threatened to descend on him.

What did it mean?

Jeff felt the uneasiness crystallize into real fear. He broke into a run down the corridor toward his room. Fear pounded through his mind, suddenly, unreasonably. He tore open the door, fell inside, closed it tight behind him before snapping on the lights.

The room was empty. The coffeepot still stood on the little table. It was still hot, still steaming. Blackie was gone and a cigarette still burned on the edge of the tray.

He had to get out! He knew it then, knew that was at the bottom of the unreasonable fear. The bell was still clanging in the hallway, loudly piercing the still air of the room. He had to flee while he could. Instinctively now he knew that he'd never find Paul Conroe in the Center, never in a thousand years of searching. The fear grew stronger, a little voice screaming in his ear, *"Don't wait. Run, run now, or it's too late."*

He tore open his footlocker, stared at the empty hooks. The locker was cleaned out, empty of every stitch of clothing. His bag was gone, his shoes, his coat.

It's too late. Don't wait.

His pulse pounded in his temples and a sweat broke out on his forehead. The escalator! If he could get to it, then make the turn into the next corridor, and get a jitney car... It was the only way to get out and he had no choice. Panting, he broke out into the hall once again, ran pell-mell down the corridor toward the escalator. Then, when he was almost there, a wire cage slammed down across the corridor and blocked his path completely.

Jeff stopped short, his shoes scraping against the concrete floor. His heart pounded a deafening tattoo in his ears as he stared at the wire grill. Then he whirled and ran back down the corridor as fast as his legs would move. If he could get back to the offices, back to the main corridor before they stopped him, he could get a car there. Far ahead he saw the bright light of the main corridor. His breath came in a hoarse whine as he tried to run faster. And then, ten yards ahead, he saw another grill clank down, cutting him off, falling directly in his path.

He cried out, a helpless, desperate cry. He was trapped, caught in the one length of corridor. His mind spun dizzily to Blackie. She had been gone. Where to? Where had everybody gone? He started back, frantically jerking open doors on either side of the corridor, staring into room after room, his breath catching in his throat as he ran. All the rooms were empty. Jeff felt his mind spinning. He felt a curious inevitability, a fantastic pattern falling into shape as he stared into the empty rooms. Finally he reached his own again. Wide-eyed and panting, he threw the door open, strode in and threw himself down in the chair and waited.

He did not wait long. For a few moments there was no sound. Then he heard the sounds of feet coming down the corridor. He tightened his grip on the chair arm. He wasn't thinking any longer. Cold beads of sweat stood out on his forehead as he waited, hearing the steps draw nearer. For the first time that he could remember, sheer terror crept through his mind, paralyzing him. He knew he had waited too long. His chance to jump the road was gone; there was no longer any escape.

Then the door was filled by some figures. One of them was the tall, white figure of Dr. Schiml. He walked into the room and smiled like the cat that ate the canary. Sinking down on the bed with a sigh, he was still smiling at Jeff. The girl followed him into the room. Her eyes were downcast. She tossed a little pair of ivory dice into the air and caught them as they fell.

The doctor smiled, and drew a crisp white paper from his pocket, began unfolding it slowly. "A matter of business," he said, almost apologetically. "It's time we got down to business, I think."

CHAPTER ELEVEN

JEFF RAISED his eyes to the doctor's face. His throat felt like sandpaper. He tried to swallow and couldn't. "Sorry," he grated. "I've changed my mind. I'm not talking business."

Dr. Schiml smiled, his head slowly moving back and forth. "I hear you're quite handy at the dice, Jeff."

Jeff jumped out of the chair, fists clenched, eyes blazing at the girl. "You bitch," he snarled. "You two-bit tramp stoolie. You'd sell your grandmother short for a bag of salt, wouldn't you? Come to me with your sob stories, beg me to move out of here with you." His voice was biting. "How much did they pay you to sell out? A hundred thousand, maybe? Or was this just a little routine affair? Maybe a thousand or two?"

The girl's face darkened, her eyes bewildered as she stared at him. "No, that's not true. I didn't—"

"Well, it won't do them any good, no matter how much they paid you. Because I'm not signing a release, now or ever."

A guard grabbed Jeff's arm, forcing him back into the chair.

Dr. Schiml still smiled, clasping his knee with his hands. "I guess you didn't quite understand me," he said pleasantly. "You mustn't blame Blackie. She didn't sell you short. She just couldn't help answering a few perfectly innocent questions." His eyes returned to Jeff, coldly. "We're not asking you to sign a release, Jeff. We're telling you."

Jeff stared at him in amazement. "Don't be silly," he blurted. "I'm not signing a release to you people. Do you think I'm out of my mind? Take it away, burn it and get yourself another guinea pig."

Dr. Schiml smiled quietly and shook his head. "We don't want another guinea pig, Jeff. That's just it. We want you."

A little line of sweat broke out on Jeff's forehead. "Look," he said hoarsely. "I'm not signing anything, do you understand? I've changed my mind. I don't care for the work here. I don't like the company."

Schiml's smile faded. He shrugged and tucked the white paper back into his white coat. "Just as you wish," he said. "The release is just a formality. Bring him along, boys."

"Wait!" Jeff was on his feet again, facing the guards, his eyes wide with fright. His eyes caught Schiml's. "Look, you've got things wrong. I'm a fake in here, a fraud. Can't you understand that? I didn't come in here to volunteer. I never intended to volunteer, never planned to go even as far as I did. I came here—"

Schiml made an impatient face and held up a hand. "Oh, yes, yes, I know all that. You came into this place because you'd followed a man in here and you wanted to kill him. You'd been hunting him for years, because you thought he murdered your father in cold blood and nothing would do but you kill him. Right?" Schiml blinked at Jeff, his voice heavy with boredom. "So you came in here and went through testing, hunting down your man, trying to find him. But you didn't find him. Now things have suddenly become too hot for your liking, so you figure that it's time to pull out. Right? Or are some of the details wrong?"

Jeff's jaw sagged, his face going pasty. "That slut girl—"

Schiml grimaced. "No, not Blackie. Blackie is discreet, in her own quiet way. She hasn't had anything to do with it. We've known about you all along, Jeff. And through a much more reliable source than Blackie." He glanced over his shoulder at one of the guards. "Bring him in," he said abruptly.

The door to the adjoining room opened and a man walked into the room. He was a tall, lean man; a gaunt-faced man with sallow cheeks and large, sad eyes; a weary-looking man whose hair was graying about the temples—a man whose whole body looked desperately tired.

And Schiml looked at the man and then he looked at the ceiling. "Hello, Paul," he said softly. "There's someone here who's been looking for you—"

A scream broke from Jeff's lips as he stared across the room. A raw animal scream ripped from his mouth like a knife. His lips twisted and he wrenched at the guards who were holding his arms, his face going purple, his eyes bulging.

With a roar he lunged at Conroe, bellowing, a torrent of hatred and abuse pouring from his lips. Again and again he screamed, his eyes blazing with an unholy fire of hatred. Conroe jerked back with a cry, and then Schiml was on his feet as Jeff lunged again, his muscles tightening like bands of steel under the flimsy shirt.

The guards fought to restrain him, and then the doctor was holding him too, crying: "Get out, Paul, quick!"

But Paul Conroe stood stock still, writhing from his hands to his head, his eyes filling with horrible pain. Suddenly the coffee cup jerked from the table, spun in the air and hurled straight for Conroe's head. It missed, smashing against the wall.

Jeff screamed again and the walls and ceiling began powdering off, plaster peeling down in great chunks, smashing, off the walls onto the floor. A huge chunk fell from the ceiling, and then the curtains suddenly started to blaze, as if ignited by some magic fire. Finally, Conroe's clothing began smoking and smoldering.

Blackie screamed, staring at Jeff in open horror. Schiml's voice roared through the bedlam: "Get him! Sedate him, for God's sake, before he tears the place down on our ears!" Again Jeff roared his virulent hatred, and this time Conroe was the one who shouted:

"Stop him! He's tearing me apart inside. My God, stop him!"

Someone stepped between Jeff and Conroe. There was a flicker of glass and silver as a plunger was pressed home. Then suddenly Jeff's muscles gave out. His legs walked out from under him, and he felt himself sliding to the floor. But still he screamed, the face of the man who had tormented him all his life growing closer and closer, more and more vicious. Then suddenly everything around him went black. His last conscious impression was that of Blackie. She had her face in her hands and she was sobbing like a child in the corner.

He lay on the long table, wrapped in cool green surgical linens, motionless, barely breathing. His eyes were wide open, but sightless. They seemed to be staring straight up at the pale, glowing skylight in the ceiling. It was as if they were staring beyond, eons beyond, into some strange world that no human foot had ever trod.

His breath came slowly, a harsh sound in the still room. Sometimes it slowed almost to a stop, sometimes it accelerated. Dr. Schiml paused motionless by his side, waiting, watching breathlessly until the ragged wheeze slowed once again to normal.

Jeff lay like a corpse, but he was not dead. Near his head the panel of tiny lights flickered on and off, brighter and dimmer, carrying their simple on-or-off messages from the myriad microscopic endings on the tiny electrode that probed through the soft brain tissue.

No human being could ever analyze the waxing and waning of patterns on that panel, not even in five lifetimes. But a camera could film the changes, instant upon instant, flickering and flashing and glowing dully on and off, in a thousand thousand different figures and movements. And the computer could take these patterns from the film and analyze them and compare them. It would integrate them into the constantly changing picture that appeared on the small screen by the bedside.

It was a crude instrument, indeed, for the study of so exquisitely delicate and variable an instrument as a human brain, and no one knew this more painfully than Roger Schiml. But even such a crude instrument could probe into that strange half-world that they had sought so long to enter.

Near the bedside Paul Conroe sat motionless, his face drawn, his gaunt cheeks sunken. His eyes were wide and fearful as he watched the picture panel and his fingers trembled as he lit his pipe. He kept watching.

"It could be so dangerous," he murmured finally, turning to look at Schiml. "So terribly dangerous."

Schiml nodded gravely, adjusting the microvernier that controlled the probing instrument. "Of course it could be dangerous, but not too much so. Twenty years ago he'd have been dead already, but we haven't been wasting time all these years we've been waiting for him. Particularly in this cell-probing technique, we've ironed out the bugs. He'll survive, all right, unless we run into something mighty—"

Conroe shook his head. "Oh, no, no. I don't mean dangerous for him. I mean dangerous for us. Even he doesn't realize his power. How can we predict what sort of power it might be?" he looked up at Schiml, his eyes wide. "That room—it would have been gone in another five minutes, simply torn apart into molecular dust. He did it—and yet, I'd swear he didn't know what he was doing. I doubt if he even realized what was happening. And the fire—that was real fire, Roger. I know, I felt it burn me."

Schiml nodded eagerly. "Of course it was real fire! Set molecules to spinning at terrifically accelerated rates and you have fire. But those are the things we have to learn, Paul."

Conroe shook his head, fearfully. "We could both see the fire, but there was something else. You couldn't feel the hatred that was in that room. I could." He looked up, his eyes haunted. "God, Roger, how could a man hate that way? It was thick; it ran out into the room like syrup. Oh, I've felt hatred before in the minds I've contacted, many times. I've felt vile hatred before, but this was alive, crawling hate—" He sighed, his hands trembling. "It's in his mind, Roger. We don't know what else he might do, even under anesthetic, if we hit the right places. But it's in his mind. That we know. But why?"

Schiml nodded again. "That's the key question, of course. Why does he hate you so much? When we know that"—the doctor spread his hands—"we'll have the answer to twenty years' work, perhaps. And dangerous as it is, we've got to find out, while we have a chance, Paul. You know that. We can't stop now, not with what we know. We know that Jeff's insanity is far less active right now than his father's was. But unless we can locate the areas, find the location of both factors, the psychosis and the extra-sensory powers, we're lost. We d have no recourse but to turn our findings over to the authorities. And you know what that would mean."

Conroe nodded wearily. "Yes, I know. Mass slaughter, sterilization, fear, panic—all the wrong answers. And even the panic alone would be fatal in our psychotic world."

Dr. Schiml shrugged and went back to the bedside. "We'll know soon, one way or the other," he said softly. "We're coming through right now."

CHAPTER TWELVE

The needle moved, probed ever so slightly, stimulating deep, deep in the soft, fragile tissue…seeking, probing, recording. A twinge, the barest trace of shock, a sharp series of firing nerve cells, a flicker of light, a picture—Jeff Meyer shifted, his eyelids lowering very slightly, and a muscle in his jaw began twitching involuntarily…

He was floating gently on his back, resting on huge, fluffy, billowing clouds. He didn't know where he was, nor did he care. He just lay still, spinning gently, like a man in free fall, feeling the gentle clouds around him pressing him downward and downward. His eyes were closed tightly—so tightly that no ray of light might leak in. He knew as he floated that whatever happened, he dare not open them.

But then there were sounds around him. He felt his muscles tighten and he clasped his chest with his arms. There were things floating through the air around him, and they were making little sounds: tiny squeaks and groans. He shuddered, suddenly horribly afraid. The noises grew louder and louder, whispering into his ear, laughing at him.

He opened his eyes with a jolt, staring at the long, black, hollow tunnel he was falling through. He was spinning, end over end, faster and faster down the tunnel. He strained to see through the darkness to the bottom, but he couldn't. Then the laughter started. First little, quiet giggles, quite near his ear, but growing louder and louder—unpleasant laughs, chuckles, guffaws. They followed each other, peal upon peal of insane laughter, reverberating from the curved tunnel walls, growing louder and louder, more and more derisive. They were laughing at him—whoever they were—and their laughs rose into screams in his ears. Then to gain silence he was forced to scream out himself. And he clasped his hands to his ears and shut his eyes tight—and abruptly the laughter stopped. *Everything* stopped.

He lay tense, listening. No, not everything. There were some sounds. Somewhere in the distance he could hear the bzz-bzz-bzz of a cicada. It sounded sharp in the summer night air. He rolled over, felt the crisp sheets under him, the soft pillow, the rustling of the light blanket. Where? …

And then it came to him, clearly. He was in his room, waiting, waiting and expecting.

Daddy! Quite suddenly, he knew that Daddy had come home. There had been no sound in the dark house; he hadn't even heard the jet-car go into the garage, nor the front door squeak. But he had known, just the same, that Daddy was here. He blinked at the darkness, and little chills of fright ran up his spine. It was so dark, and he didn't like the dark, and he wished Daddy would come up and turn on the light. But Daddy had said ever since Mommy died that he must be a brave little man, even if he was only four…

He lay and shivered. There were other noises: outside the window, in the room—frightening noises. It was all very well to be a brave little man, but Daddy just didn't understand about the dark and the noises. And Daddy didn't understand about how he wanted somebody to hold him close and cuddle him and whisper to him.

And then he heard Daddy's step on the stair and felt him coming nearer. He rolled over and giggled, pretending to be asleep. Not that he'd fool Daddy for a minute. Daddy would already know he was awake. They played the same game night after night. But it was fun to play little games like that with Daddy. He waited, listening until he heard the door open, and the footsteps reach his bed. He heard Daddy's breathing. And then he rolled over and threw the covers off and jumped up like a little white ghost, shouting, "Boo! Did I scare you, Daddy?"

And then Daddy took him up on his shoulders and laughed, and said he was a big white horse come to carry little Jeff on a long journey. So they took the long journey down to the study for milk and cookies, just as they always did when Daddy came home. He knew Daddy didn't want any milk, of course. Daddy never drank milk at night with him. Daddy was much more interested in the funny cards, the cards he had watched Daddy make that day a year ago. Daddy had him run through them over and over and over...circle, spiral, figure eight, letter B, letter R... *It was a letter R, Daddy? But it couldn't have been, I know—oh, you're trying to catch me! Can we play with the marbles now, Daddy? Or the dice tonight? The round-cornered ones—they're much easier, you know.*

But Daddy would watch him as he read the cards, wrinkling up his nose and calling out the figure. And he would see Daddy mark down each right one and each wrong one. And then he would feel Daddy almost beaming happiness and satisfaction. And he would wait eagerly for Daddy to get out the dice, because they were so much more fun than the cards. *The square-cornered dice, Daddy? Oh, Daddy, they're so much harder. Oh, another game, a new one? Oh, good, Daddy. Teach me a new game with them, please. I'll try very hard to make them come out right.*

And then after the new game, Daddy told him a story before bed. It was one of his funny stories, where he talked the story, but put in all the fun and jokes and private things without any words.

It was funny. None of the others, like Mary Ann down the block, could feel their daddies like he could. Sometimes he wondered about it. He would tell Mary Ann about it as a special secret, but she wouldn't believe him. Nobody can hear their daddies without their daddies talking, she said. But he knew better.

And then there were thoughts creeping through his mind, feelings coming from Daddy that were uncomfortable feelings. He sat up suddenly in Daddy's arms and felt the chill pass through him.

"Daddy…"

"Yes, son."

"Why are you afraid, Daddy? What are you afraid of?"

And Daddy laughed and looked at him in a strange way and said, "Afraid? What do you mean, afraid?" But the afraidness was still there. Even when he went to bed and Daddy left him again, he could still feel the afraidness…

And then, abruptly, he was swinging into a vast, roaring whirlpool that swung around his head. He felt his body twisting in the blackness, swirling about, carried along without effort. He knew, somehow, that he was Jeff Meyer. And he knew that the needle was there, probing in his mind; he could feel it approach and withdraw. He could feel the twinge of recognition, the almost intangible sudden awareness and realization of a truth.

Then the seeker was gone: the probe finished in that area and moved on to the next. The whirlpool was a tunnel of rushing water, swinging about him, whirling him with lightning speed up…up…up; around, then down with a sickening rush. Then up again, as though he were riding the Wall of Death in a circus, around and around…yet always drawing him in closer…closer…closer…

To what?

He knew he was fighting it, twisting with all his strength to fight against the impossible whirlpool that choked and carried him like a feather. He clenched his fists and fought, gritting his teeth, desperate, suddenly horribly afraid, more horribly afraid than he had ever been in his life. Down at the end of the tumultuous whirlpool, something lay—something horrid and ugly, something that had been wiped out of his mind, scoured out and disposed of long, long ago. *It was something he dared not face, never again.* Suddenly Jeff screamed and tried to force his mind back to that place. He tried desperately to remember, tried to see where the whirlpool was leading him before it was too late—*before it killed him!*

Something lay down there, waiting for him. It was more hideous than his mind could *imagine—something that could kill him.* Closer and closer he swept, helpless, his body growing rigid with fear, fighting, blood rushing through his veins. But he couldn't escape that closed, frantic alleyway to death.

Daddy was afraid. The thought screamed through Jeff's mind with the impact of a lightning bolt. It paralyzed his thoughts, tightened his muscles into rigid knots. Daddy was afraid...afraid...*afraid*—so horribly afraid.

The thought swept through him, congealing his blood. He cried out, shaking his head, trying to fight away the seeping stench of deadly fear, trying to clear it out of his mind. His face twisted in agony and his whole body wrenched. Suddenly, he was screaming and pounding his face against the ground. He was alone and his mind was wracked and obsessed by that horrible fear.

He opened his eyes and saw the turf under his head. Dimly, through the pain sweeping through his mind, he saw the grassy meadow on which he lay, completely by himself. The little singing brook was a few feet away. The afternoon sun was high, but the willow tree hung over him, covering him with cool shade. From somewhere a bird was singing.

"Daddy!" The word broke from his lips in a small scream, and he sat bolt upright, his hair tousled, his small, keen-featured eight-year-old face twisted with the pain and fear that tore through his mind. Some corner of his brain, so very remote, told him that he was not eight, that he was a grown man. But he saw his tiny hands, grubby with the dirt of the barnyard and lane through which he had walked in coming here. He had been driven here by the pain and fear and hatred that had been streaming into his mind.

It was Daddy. He knew it was Daddy, and Daddy was afraid. Daddy was running, with the desperation of a hunted animal, running down a corridor, his mind in a frenzy of fear. He was peering back over his shoulder, his breath coming in great gasps as he reached the end of the hall, wrenched vainly at the door and then collapsed against it. And while he sobbed in great gasps, tears of fear and desperation ran down his cheeks.

Jeff saw the door; he felt Daddy's body heaving, heard the furious pulse pounding in his own head. He saw the cold, darkened corridor, and his mind was picked up in the frenzied sweep of his father's thoughts, carried in a rush he could neither understand nor oppose. Stronger than ever before, his thoughts were Daddy's thoughts. He saw through Daddy's eyes; he felt through Daddy's body. In the closest rapport they had ever known, though Jeff lay here on the grassy plot, his body writhed with the pain and fear that Daddy was suffering miles distant.

They're coming, his mind screamed. *Trapped, trapped—what can I do?* Daddy was racing back up the corridor now, his eye catching an elevator standing open. He ran inside, groped frantically for the switch. He had to get away, had to get down below, somehow get to the street! Oh what a mistake to walk into this place—an office building, of all places, where they could easily follow him in, cut him off, trap him!

Why had he come? Why? He'd known they were hunting

for him, knew they'd been getting closer and closer. But how could he have sensed that this day would bring a panic, that the stock market would take its nosedive this one particular day, putting the finger on him without any question, spotting him, pointing out his exact location to his hunters, beyond shadow of doubt?

How could he have known? This was to have been the final test to prove the force he had in his mind—the force that had been destroying and destroying and destroying. And it had emanated from his own mind in some unspeakable way, uncontrolled, unbelieved and misunderstood. It was the force that had brought the hunters to him.

But not now! Oh, please, please, not now—not when he was so close to the answer. Not when he was so close. Slowly, helpless anger seethed through his mind. They had no right to stop him now. In another day, another week, he could have the answer. In another few days he would have corralled this frightening power, controlled it. He knew he could find the answer. He stood on the very brink. But now the hunters had trapped him—

Why, Daddy? Why are they hunting you? Oh, Daddy, Daddy, please, I'm so scared! Please, Daddy, come home. Please don't be so much afraid, Daddy. I'm so frightened…

The elevator gave a lurch. He fell against the door as the car ground to a halt between floors. Frantically, he pounded the button, waited through long eternities as the car sat, silent, motionless. Then his fingers ran hastily along the cracks in the car door, seeking a hold, trying desperately to wrench open the locked door.

He felt them coming, somewhere above him, somewhere below him. Then something tore loose in his mind; some last dam of control broke, and he was screaming his defiance at them, screaming his hatred, his bitterness. They had him, they were going to kill him without trial, shoot him down like a mad dog. He felt them flinch and cower back at the stream of hatred roaring out of his mind, felt them move back. They were afraid of him, but they were determined to kill him.

A sound above! He flattened back against the elevator wall, wrenching at the metal grating with superhuman strength, trying to twist open the metal, to find some way into the shaft below. Someone was coming down from above, down onto the top of the elevator; someone whose mind was filled with fear, but who moved with determination. There was a scraping sound from above, a dull twang of cable striking against cable.

They could be cutting the car loose.

He leaped for the ceiling of the car, stabbing up with his fingers for the little escape doorway. Sheer hatred drove his legs as he jumped and jumped again, until the door flew up. His hand caught the rim, and he dragged his body up. He jerked his shoulders through the small opening, heaving and lunging through to the top of the car.

He looked up. He saw a face, a single face, hanging mistily above him. Dimly he made out the form of a man hanging on the cable twenty feet above. His legs were wrapped around the cables and one hand carried the small, dully gleaming weapon. His mind screamed hatred at the man, and he grabbed at the cables, wrenching them, shaking them like a huge tree. He saw the man slowly moving down, spinning back and forth helplessly as the cables vibrated. But he held on tenaciously, moving closer.

Daddy! Stop him! Daddy, don't let him kill you.

The face came into clearer view: a thin face, an evil one, twisted with fear and pain. The figure moved slowly down the cables, slowly turning, lifting the arm with the weapon, patiently trying to take aim. It was a gaunt face, with high cheekbones, slightly bulging eyes, high flat forehead, graying hair. *Remember that face, Jeff. Never forget that face, that face is the face of the man who is butchering your father.* Hatred streamed out at the face; he crouched back against the wall of the shaft, wrenching at the cables, trying vainly to shake the killer loose. He had to get him first; he had to stop him. *He's so close; he's turning; the gun is raising. I'll never get him—*

The face, hovering close, eyes wide—the face of a ghoul—and below the face was the dull, round hole of the gun muzzle, just inches away. A finger tightened. A horrible flash came, straight in the eyes—

Daddy!

The thoughts screamed through his mind: the bitter, naked hatred, the hatred of madness, streaming out in one last searing inferno. Then came a sickening lurch, a lurch of maddened fear and hate. And there was the snuffing out of a light, leaving darkness...

Daddy! No, Daddy. No, I can't feel you any more, Daddy. What have they done to you? Oh, please, Daddy, talk to me. Talk to me. No, no, no. Oh, Daddy, Daddy, Daddy...

Dr. Schiml looked up from the pale, prostrate form after a long time; his forehead was beaded with sweat. The color had drained almost completely from Jeff's face, and his skin had taken a waxy cast. His breathing was so shallow it was hardly audible in the still room, and the panel of flickering lights had become almost completely still.

"We can't go on yet," said Dr. Schiml, his voice hoarse. "We'll have to wait." He turned and walked across the room, trying to keep his eyes away from the prostrate form on the bed; yet everywhere he went, it seemed his eyes caught the idiotic stare in the man's blank eyes. "We'll have to wait," he repeated, and his voice was almost a sob.

CHAPTER THIRTEEN

PAUL CONROE moved for the first time, running a hand through his thick gray hair as he glanced up at Schiml.

"Some of that came through to me, even now," he said weakly. His face, also, was ashen and his eyes were haunted. "To think that he hated me that much, and to think why he hated me—" He shook his head and buried his face in his hands. "I never knew about the old man and the son. I just never knew. If I'd known, I'd never have done it."

The room was still for a long moment. Then Schiml blinked at Conroe, his hands trembling. "So this is the tremendous power, the mutant strain we've been trying to trace for so long."

"This is one of the tremendous powers," Conroe replied wearily. "Jeff probably has all the power that his father had, though it hasn't all matured yet. It's just latent, waiting for the time that the genes demand of his body for fulfillment. Nothing more. And other people have the same powers. Hundreds, thousands of other people. Somewhere, a hundred and fifty years ago, there was a change—a little change in one man or one woman."

He looked up at Schiml, the haunted look still in his large eyes. "Extra-sensory powers—no doubt of it, a true mutant strain, but tied in to a sleeper—a black gene that spells insanity. One became two and two spread to four-extra-sensory power and gene-linked insanity. Always together, growing, insidiously growing like a cancer. And it's eating out the roots of our civilization."

He stood up, walked across the room and, stared down at the pallid-faced man in the bed. "This answers so many things, Roger," he said finally. "We knew old Jacob Meyer had a son, of course. We even suspected then that the son might share some of his powers. But this! We never dreamed it. The father and son were practically two people with one mind, in almost perfect mutual rapport. Only the son was so young he couldn't understand what was wrong. All he knew was that he 'felt' Daddy and could tell what

Daddy was thinking. Actually, everything that went on in his father's mind—*everything*—was in his mind too. At least, in the peak of the old man's cycle of insanity—"

Schiml looked up sharply. "Then there's no doubt in your mind that the old man was insane?"

Conroe shook his head. "Oh, no. There was no doubt. He was insane, all right. A psychiatric analysis of his behavior was enough to convince me of that, even if following him and watching him wasn't. He had a regular cycle of elation and depression, so regular it could almost be clocked. He'd even spotted the symptoms of the psychosis himself, back in his college days. But of course he hadn't realized what it was. All he knew was that at certain times he seemed to be surrounded by these peculiar phenomena, which happened rapidly and regularly at those times when he was feeling elated, on top of the world. And at other times he seemed to carry with him an aura of depression. Actually, when he hit the blackest depths of his depressions, he would be bringing about whole waves of suicides and depression-errors and everything else."

Conroe took a deep breath. "We knew all this at the time, of course. What we didn't know was that the old man had been seeking the answer himself, actively seeking it. All we knew was that he was actively the most dangerous man alive on Earth, and that until he was killed he would become more and more dangerous—dangerous enough to shake the very roots of our civilization."

Schiml nodded slowly. "And you're sure that his destructive use of his power was a result directly of the insanity?"

Conroe frowned. "Not quite," he said after a moment. "Actually, you couldn't say that Jacob Meyer 'used' his extra-sensory powers. They weren't, for the most part, the kind of powers he could either control or 'use.' They were the sort of powers that just happened. He had a power, and when he was running high—in a period of elation, when everything was on top of the world—the power functioned. He fairly exuded this power that he carried, and the higher he rose in his elation, the more viciously dangerous the power became.

Conroe stopped, staring at the bed for a long moment. "The hellish thing was that it couldn't possibly be connected up with a human power at all. After all, how can one human being have an overwhelming effect on the progress of a business cycle? He can't, of course, unless he's a dictator, or a tremendously powerful person in some other field. And Jacob Meyer was neither. He was a simple, half-starved statistician with a bunch of ideas that he couldn't even understand himself, much less sell to anyone who could do anything with them. Or how can a man, *just by being in the vicinity*, tip the balance that topples the stock market into an almost irreparable sag?"

Conroe leaned forward, groping for words. "Jacob Meyer's psychokinesis was not the sort of telekinesis that we saw Jeff turning against me in that room a couple of hours ago. He could probably have managed that, too, if he had hated me enough. But if Jacob Meyer's mind had merely affected physical things—the turn of a card, the fall of the dice, the movement of molecules from one place to another—he would have been a simple problem. We could have isolated him, studied him. But it wasn't that simple."

Paul Conroe sat back, regarding Schiml with large, sad eyes. "It would have been impossible to prove in a court of law. We knew it and the government knew it. That was why they appointed us assassins to deal with him. *Because Jacob Meyer's mind affected probabilities.* By his very presence, in a period of elation, he upset the normal probabilities of occurrences going on around him. We watched him, Roger. It was incredible. We watched him in the stock market, and we saw the panic start almost the moment he walked in. We saw the buyers suddenly and inexplicably change their minds and start selling instead of buying. We saw what happened in the Bank of the Metropolis that first day we tried for him. He was scared, his mind was driven into a peak of fear and anger; it started a bank run that morning that nearly bankrupted the most powerful financial house on the East Coast! We saw this one little man's personal, individual influence on international diplomacy, on finances, on gambling in Reno, on the thinking and acting of the man on the street. It was incredible, Roger."

"But surely Jacob Meyer wasn't the only one——"

"Oh, there were others, certainly. We've a better idea of that, now, after all these years of study. There were and are thousands and thousands—some like me, some much worse—all carrying some degree of extra-sensory power from that original mutant strain, all with the gene-linked psychosis paired up with it every time. And we've seen our civilization struggling against these thousands just to keep its feet. But Jacob Meyer was the first case of the whole, full-blown change in one man that we'd ever found. He was running wild, his mind was completely insane. And the extra-sensory powers he carried were so firmly enmeshed in the insanity that there was no separating the two. Meyer tipped us off. He set us on the trail, and the trail led to his son after he was dead——"

"Yes, the son. We have the son." Schiml scowled at the shallow-breathing form on the bed. "We should have had him before—years before."

"Of course we should. But the son vanished after his father's death. We never knew why he vanished—until now. But now we know that when we killed his father, we did more than just that. We almost killed our last chance to catch this thing and study it before it was too late. Because when we killed Jeff's father, *we killed Jeff Meyer too.*"

Schiml scowled. "I don't follow. He's still alive."

"Oh, of course he's still alive. But can't you see what happened to him? He was living in his father's mind; he knew everything his father knew—but he didn't understand it. He thought with his father's thoughts, he saw through his father's eyes, because they were mutually and completely telepathic. He felt his father's fear and frustration and bitterness when we trapped him in that office building finally. He lay screaming on the ground on a farm somewhere, but actually he was in his father's mind.

"It was a mad mind, a mind rising to the highest screaming heights of mania, as he waited for me to come down and kill him. And Jeff was surrounded with his father's hatred. He saw my face through his father's eyes, and all he could understand was that his daddy was being butchered and that I was butchering him. When the bullet went into his father's brain and split his skull open, Jeff Meyer felt that too. When his father died, Jeff died too—a part of him, that is. They were one mind and part of that one mind was destroyed."

Conroe paused, his forehead covered with sweat. The room was silent except for the hoarse breathing of the man on the table. Conroe's face, as he looked down, was that of a ghost.

"No wonder the boy disappeared," he whispered. "He'd been shot through the head. He was almost virtually dead. He must have gone into shock for years after such a trauma, Roger. He must have spent years roaming that farm, cared for by an aunt or uncle or cousin, while he slowly recovered. No wonder we could find no trace. And then, when he did get well, all he knew was that his father had been murdered. He didn't know how; he didn't know why, and he dared never remember the truth. Because the truth was that *he* had been killed. All he dared recognize was my face—a recurrent, nightmarish hallucination, rising out of his dreams, plaguing him on the streets, tormenting him day and night."

"But you were hunting him."

"Oh, yes, we were hunting him. It was inevitable that sooner or later we would come up face to face. But when we did, I received such a horrible mental blow that I couldn't even look to see what he looked like. I could do nothing but scream and run. When he saw me that day in the nightclub, he took complete leave of his senses. He exploded into hatred and bitterness. And then he resolved to hunt me down and kill me for killing his father."

Conroe spread his hands apologetically. "It seemed good sense to use that hatred and singleness of purpose to draw him here. But it was torture. He followed me with his mind, without knowing it. It was old Jacob Meyer's face that haunted me everywhere I went. I didn't know why, then, because I didn't know Jeff had been part of that mind. And Jeff didn't know that he carried and broadcast that horror where he went."

Conroe leaned back, his body limp in exhaustion. "We needed Jeff so desperately. Yes, we needed him in here, for testing, for this study. It's been a long, tedious job, studying him, observing him, photographing him, learning how much of his father's power he had. And we dared not bring him in here until we were sure it was safe. And now, with what he knows, he is more vitally dangerous than his father ever was. There are hundreds that carry the change, in larger or smaller part, all gene-linked with insanity. And Jeff Meyer is insane as any of the rest of them. But at least there's hope, because we can study him now. Because unless we can somehow separate the function of the insanity from the function of the psychokinesis, we have no choice left, no hope."

Schiml looked up, his eyes wide. "No choice—"

"—but to kill them, every one. To hunt out the strain and wipe it from the face of the Earth so ruthlessly and completely that it can never rise again. And to wipe out with it the first new link in the evolution of Man since the dawn of history."

Slowly Schiml's eyes traveled from Jeff Meyers' form on the bed to Paul Conroe's grave face. "There's no other way?"

"None," said Paul Conroe.

"Jeff," said Dr. Schiml. "Jeff Meyer."

The figure on the cot stirred ever so slightly. The eyes slowly closed, then reopened, looking slightly less blank. Jeff's lips parted in an inaudible groan, hardly more than a breath.

"Jeff. You've got to hear me a minute. Listen, Jeff, we're trying to help you. Can you hear that? We're trying to help you, Jeff, and we need your help."

The eyes shifted, turned to Schiml's face. They were haunted eyes—eyes that had seen the grave and beyond it.

"Please, Jeff. Listen. We're hunting. We're trying to find a way to help you. You know about your father now, the truth about your father, don't you?"

The eyes wavered, came back, and the head nodded ever so slightly. "I know," came the sighing reply.

"You've got to tell us what to do, Jeff. There are good powers here in your mind, and there are terrible powers, ruinous powers. We've got to find them both, find where they lie, how they work. You must tell us, as we probe—tell us when we strike the good, when we strike the bad. Do you understand, Jeff?"

Again the head nodded. Jeff's jaw tightened a trifle and an expression of infinite fatigue crossed his face. "Go on, Doc."

Dr. Schiml leaned over the proper controls and moved the dial on the microvernier. He moved it again, watching, moving it still again. A fine sweat broke out on his forehead as he worked, and he felt Conroe's soft eyes on him, waiting, hoping.

And then a whimper broke from Jeff's lips, an indefinable sound, helpless and childlike, a little cry of terror. Dr. Schiml looked up, his heart thumping in his throat. Jeff's eyes were wide again, staring lifelessly, and his breath was shallow and thready. Schiml glanced quickly at Conroe, then back, his eyes reflecting the fear and tension in his mind. And as he worked his shoulders slumped forward, prepared for defeat. Because what he was doing was impossible, and he knew it was impossible. But he knew, above all, that it had to succeed.

CHAPTER FOURTEEN

HE WAS spinning like a top, end over end, as though he had sprung off a huge, powerful diving board. He rose higher and higher into the air. Lying tense, Jeff knew that his body was still on the soft bed, yet he felt his feet rising, his head sinking, as he spun head over heels through the blackness. And he could feel the tiny probing needle, seeking, hunting, stimulating...

A siren noise burst in his ears: a shimmering blast of screeching musical sound that sent cold shivers down his back. Then it leveled off to an up-and-down whine that gradually became a blat of static in his ear. Somewhere, out of the uneven grating of the noise, he heard a voice whispering in his ear, hoarsely. He paused, straining to hear, trying to catch an occasional word.

He knew that there were no voices outside of his body. He was sure of that. Yet he heard the sound, deeper in his ear, louder and softer, then louder again. It whispered to him, with a note of deepest urgency in the soft sibilants. Quite suddenly, it seemed vitally important to hear what the voice was saying, for the words were clearly directed at him. He shifted slightly and listened harder, until the words came through clearly.

And then he gasped, a feeling of panic sweeping through him. He heard the words and they were nonsense words, sounds without meanings. Something stirred in his mind, some vague memory of nonsense words, of a horrible shock. Had there been a shock? But the strange sounds frightened him, driving fear down through the marrow of his bones. The whispering sounds were sinister: babbling sounds, sounds of words that *needed* meaning and had none---half--words, garbled, twisted, meaningless.

Cautiously he opened his eyes, peered through the murky

blackness to see the whisperers. His eyes fastened on two shapeless forms, tall, ghostly, in black robes with hoods drawn up over their faces. The figures leaned on their sticks and held their heads together. They babbled nonsense to each other with such fierce earnestness that they seemed somehow horridly ridiculous. Taking a deep breath, Jeff started toward the two figures, then stopped short, his heart pounding wildly in his throat.

Because the moment he had made a move toward them, the figures turned sharply toward him, and their nonsense voices had suddenly become clear for the briefest moment. They became clear and unmistakable and heavy with horrible meaning: "Stay away, Jeff Meyer. Stay away."

He stared about, trembling, trying to place himself, trying to find some landmark. The hooded figures turned back to each other and began babbling once again. But now they seemed to be standing before an archway—a gloomy, gray archway that they seemed to be guarding. Slowly, slyly, Jeff started to move away from them. But he watched them from stealthy eyes, and as he moved away the gloom about him cleared, and things were suddenly brighter. And then there was singing in his ears, joyous choruses bursting forth in happy song. A great feeling of relief and complacency settled down upon him like a mantle. He smiled and breathed deeper and started to roll over.

"What was that, Jeff? What did we strike?"

He shook his head violently, a frown creasing his face. "Stay away," he muttered. "The old men, they were there." Suddenly he felt himself twist around until he was facing the hooded figures again, and his feet were moving him toward them again, involuntarily, inexorably. And then the nonsense words settled out again, more menacingly, louder this time than before: "No closer, Jeff Meyer. Stay away—away—away."

"Can't go there," he muttered aloud.

"Why not, Jeff?"

"They won't let me. I've got to stay away."

"What are they guarding, Jeff?"

"I don't know, I tell you. I've got to stay away."

And then suddenly the singing dissolved into a hideous cacophony of clashing sounds, a din that nearly deafened him. A huge wave suddenly swept up around him. It was like a breaker at the ocean's edge, swirling up, surrounding him, catching him up and hurling him head over heels down a long, whirling tunnel. Desperately he fought for balance and finally found his feet under him once again. But then the ground was moving under him. He ran frantically, until his breath came in short gasps and his blood pounded in his ears. Then he caught a branch that swept by near him, and raised himself up as the flooding water roared underneath him.

The sky around him was clouding over blackly. Far in the distance he saw a blinding flash of lightning, ripping through the sky, bringing the bleak, wind-torn landscape into sharp relief in his mind as he clung to the branch. He heard a flapping of wings as a huge, black vulture skimmed by. And then the rain began to fall, a cold, soaking rain that ate through his clothes and soaked his skin. It ran in torrents into his eyes and ears and mouth.

And then he heard voices all around him. How could there be voices here? For there were no people, no sign of warm-blooded life. But there were voices, pleasant ones. They came from all sides. He could see no one, but he could feel them.

Feel them! He gasped in pure joy, shooting out his mind eagerly, unbelievingly, searching out the sudden feeling of perfect, warm contact he had just felt. And then his mind was running from person to person, dozens of persons, and he could feel them all, as clearly, as wondrously as he had ever felt his father—sharply, beautifully.

He cried out, he cried out for joy. Tears of unrelieved happiness rolled down his cheeks as he stretched out his mind and embraced the thoughts of the people he could feel but not see. And he felt his own thoughts being met, being caught and embraced and understood.

"Right here!" he shouted. "Schiml, this is it, don't lose it, man. This is the center. I'm controlling it. You've got it now. *Work it, Schiml. Work it for all you've got.*"

And then he looked at the black, menacing sky around him, and his mind laughed and cried out for the clouds to go away. And there was a wild whirling of clouds and they broke, and the sun was streaming down upon him suddenly. He threw himself from the tree, ran down the hillside. He felt a wonderful, overpowering freedom he had never felt before, his mind free to soar and soar without hindrance. There was nothing now to stand between it and complete understanding of all men. It was a mind that could go wherever he wanted it to go, do whatever he wished.

He ran down toward the bottom of the hill and felt his control growing with every step he took. He knew when he reached the bottom of the hill that the battle would be won, so he ran all the faster.

And then, like some horrible nightmare, the hooded figures loomed up directly in his path, long bony fingers stabbing out at him accusingly. He fell flat on his face at the overpowering warning in the voices that struck him. And he lay at the feet of the figures and sobbed, his whole body shaking with bitter, hopeless sobs. And the dark clouds gathered again. He was too late, too late.

"What are they guarding, Jeff?"

"I don't know. I don't know. I can't break through."

"You've got to, Jeff. You've got to! We've got the extra-sensory center. We've found it, but something is blocking it. Jeff, something is keeping you away. You've got to see what—"

"I can't. Oh, I can't. Please, don't make me!"

"You must, Jeff!"

"No!"

"Go on, Jeff."

He stood up, facing the hood figures, cowering, his whole body trembling. Deep in his mind he could feel the probing needle, moving, slowly moving, forcing him nearer and nearer to the grim figures. Slowly his feet moved, dragging in fear, a paralyzing fear that demanded every ounce of strength he possessed to make his legs function. And the voices, laden with menace, were grating in his ear, "Stay out, stay away. If you want to live, stay away...away...away..."

He moved closer and closer to the hooded figures, leaned forward to peer around them toward the gray, ghastly gate they guarded—a gate heavy with mold and rusty iron braces.

And then he reached up and threw back the hood of the first figure, stared at the face it had covered, and burst into a scream.

It was his own face!

He turned and threw back the other hood and peered intently, fighting to see the face before the features blurred out beyond recognition. It was his face, too, unmistakable. With a roar of anger and frustration he reached out, tore away the hoods, ripped them off, one with each hand, and wrenched away the enclosing shrouds.

The figures were skeletons with his face! He struck them and they shattered like thin glass, falling down in pieces at his feet. And he brushed his feet through the debris and turned to press his shoulder against the gate, heaving against it until it swung open, creaking on rusty hinges. It swung open—*on the face of madness.*

He screamed twice, frantic screams, as he tried to hide his eyes from the rotten, writhing horror behind the gate.

"Here!" he screamed. "It's here. You're at the right place. This is what you're looking for. Cut it out. Slice it away. Please, I can't stand it any longer."

His feet moved through the horrible gate, into the swarming, loathsome, horror-ridden madness that lay beyond.

And he screamed again as he saw the bright flash. He felt the wrenching, sickening lurch that took him and threw him to the ground, down the long, twisting channels of darkness, as the pain struck through his head.

Suddenly there was another blinding flash, and he felt his muscles and his mind crumble into dust. He fell and quivered and lay helplessly, as his mind sifted and drained away into the porous earth beneath him.

When he opened his eyes, he saw Conroe's face. He was tense for a moment, every muscle going into spasm. Then suddenly he relaxed and blinked and stared up at Conroe's face, his eyes filled with wonder.

"I'm sorry, Jeff. I don't know the words to tell you how sorry." There were tears in Conroe's eyes; Jeff watched them and felt a chill of wonder down his spine. For Conroe was not using words at all and yet he *knew* what Conroe wanted to say.

Wordlessly he reached up, took the man's hand, pressed it briefly and let it fall on the blanket again. "There aren't those kinds of words," he murmured.

"And you feel all right?"

Jeff blinked, sudden wonder dawning in his eyes. "I—I—I'm alive!" He struggled to sit up, felt the twinge of pain shoot down his spine.

Schiml moved up to the bedside and gently eased him back into the softness of the bed. "Yes," he said happily, "you're alive. And you're well. And there's no irony in calling you a Mercy Man." His eyes gleamed in happy triumph. "You're a whole man, Jeff—the way you were intended to be—for the first time in your life."

The words came to him clearly, yet Jeff knew not a single word had been audible in the room. "Just like my father," he murmured. "I just felt him, just knew what he was thinking."

Tears were running down Schiml's cheeks, and his face was so infinitely happy that he hardly seemed the same man. He raised a finger, silently pointed to the water glass on the table and looked at Jeff. Jeff turned his eyes to the glass, and it rose half an inch from the table and hung there, glowing slightly in the dim light of the room. Then it gently set back on the stand.

"Control," Jeff said softly. "I have control."

"The power was chained down to something else," Schiml said softly. "You had the extra-sensory power, yes, but it was linked to something that would have prevented you from ever gaining control. A degenerative insanity, part and parcel of the extra-sensory power. You're not alone, Jeff. There are many hundreds like you, in greater or lesser degrees. Conroe is like you, to a very limited extent. And he's been seeking a way to separate the two, for years. That's why you're really a Mercy Man. We knew there were two centers, but we knew no way to separate them. We had to have you to guide us, Jeff. We had to find the center of insanity in your brain to cut it out and deliver you. That's what we've waited twenty years for. And you're free, now. It's gone. And now we have a technique we can use to free a thousand others like you."

Jeff stared at them wonderingly. Sunlight streamed in the window. Across the way, he could see the ward-towers of the Hoffman Medical Center, white and gleaming. He took a deep breath of the fresh air and turned again to the two men standing by the bedside.

"Then it was you who were hunting me," he murmured. "Strange, isn't it. It wasn't me hunting Conroe. It was my father, the ghost of my father still in my mind. The ghost of a madman—" His eyes narrowed and he stared at Schiml closely. "Then there were others who knew too. Blackie knew. She must have been the girl in the night club."

"She was. A little heavy makeup, a little light plastic, those made enough change to deceive you. But she never knew why. Hypnotics can be powerful and they can erase all memory." He paused, smiling at Jeff. "Blackie will be next. We need her so much in the work we have to do, almost as much as we need you. But you've freed Blackie too. She'll be happier than she's ever been since the cloak of bad luck began broadcasting from her mind ten years ago. She'll be happier by far."

Hours later, Jeff woke again in the still room. The men were gone and the shadows were lengthening in the room, and his mind was filled with many thoughts.

"You can go if you want," Paul Conroe had said before they left. "Or you can stay, as you see fit. If you go, we can't stop you. But we beg you to stay. We need you so very much."

There would be others staying, Jeff thought. The Nasty Frenchman would stay—sneering, laughing, hating—aiming at the big money that always lurked in the future, unaware completely of the errand of mercy he was running with his life. And Harpo would stay, and all the others…

And Blackie would stay too. Poor, helpless Blackie—beautiful Blackie, desperate Blackie. For her there was a new lease. And there was no way of telling the person she would be after the new lease was signed for her.

And Conroe would stay, delivered after all these years of the burden he carried.

Wearily, yet happily, Jeff stared at the ceiling. He breathed deeply of the quiet air, his mind filled with a maze of wondering thoughts. He knew that thinking now was useless, that there really wasn't any issue any more.

He knew, as he closed his eyes again, that Jeff Meyer would stay, too.

THE END

If you've enjoyed this book, you will not want to miss these terrific titles...

ARMCHAIR SCI-FI & HORROR DOUBLE NOVELS, $12.95 each

D-1   **THE GALAXY RAIDERS** by William P. McGivern
SPACE STATION #1 by Frank Belknap Long

D-2   **THE PROGRAMMED PEOPLE** by Jack Sharkey
SLAVES OF THE CRYSTAL BRAIN by William Carter Sawtelle

D-3   **YOU'RE ALL ALONE** by Fritz Leiber
THE LIQUID MAN by Bernard C. Gilford

D-4   **CITADEL OF THE STAR LORDS** by Edmond Hamilton
VOYAGE TO ETERNITY by Milton Lesser

D-5   **IRON MEN OF VENUS** by Don Wilcox
THE MAN WITH ABSOLUTE MOTION by Noel Loomis

D-6   **WHO SOWS THE WIND...** by Rog Phillips
THE PUZZLE PLANET by Robert A. W. Lowndes

D-7   **PLANET OF DREAD** by Murray Leinster
TWICE UPON A TIME by Charles L. Fontenay

D-8   **THE TERROR OUT OF SPACE** by Dwight V. Swain
QUEST OF THE GOLDEN APE by Ivar Jorgensen and Adam Chase

D-9   **SECRET OF MARRACOTT DEEP** by Henry Slesar
PAWN OF THE BLACK FLEET by Mark Clifton.

D-10 **BEYOND THE RINGS OF SATURN** by Robert Moore Williams
A MAN OBSESSED by Alan E. Nourse

ARMCHAIR SCIENCE FICTION CLASSICS, $12.95 each

C-1   **THE GREEN MAN**
by Harold M. Sherman

C-2   **A TRACE OF MEMORY**
By Keith Laumer

C-3   **INTO PLUTONIAN DEPTHS**
by Stanton A. Coblentz

ARMCHAIR MASTERS OF SCIENCE FICTION SERIES, $16.95 each

M-1   **MASTERS OF SCIENCE FICTION, Vol. One**
Bryce Walton—"Dark of the Moon" and other tales

M-2   **MASTERS OF SCIENCE FICTION, Vol. Two**
Jerome Bixby—"One Way Street" and other tales